MW00789622

Pa-Pro-Vi Publishing presents...

"Suited For Service"

Stories by the Unsung Heroes of the Brotherhood!

~Vaughn Ward~ Janet Douglas~
~David Patterson ~Gwen Marshall~
~James Parks~ Barry Mixon~
~Donald Davis~ Veronica Gadsden~
~Bob Belcher~

Edited by Kimberly D. Parks

Suited For Service

Stories by the Unsung Heroes of the Brotherhood

An Anthology

Pa-Pro-Vi Publishing:
www.paprovipublishing.com

ISBN# 978-1-7374348-5-6

DEDICATION

There are a variety of reasons that individuals choose to join the military. Some join to find a purpose or learn a skill while others might join as a sense of patriotic duty or a desire to serve their country. Regardless the reason, because of their sacrifice, we are able to enjoy the civil liberties that we hold so dearly. This book is dedicated to every man and woman across every branch of the military who chose to wear the uniform. On behalf of Pa-Pro-Vi Publishing Company LLC, we thank YOU for YOUR service!

CONTENTS

IN MEMORY OF 9/11

"Even the smallest act of service, the simplest act of kindness, is a way to honor those we lost, a way to reclaim that spirit of unity that followed 9/11."
President Obama

"If we learn nothing else from this tragedy, we learn that life is short and there is no time for hate."
Sandy Dahl, wife of Flight 93 pilot **Jason Dahl**, in Shanksville, Pennsylvania, in 2002

"It was the worst day we have ever seen, but it brought out the best in all of us."
Senator **John Kerry**

"On this day... 20 years (September 10th) ago, 246

people went to sleep in preparation for their morning flights. 2,606 people went to sleep in preparation for work in the morning. 343 firefighters went to sleep in preparation for their morning shift. 60 police officers went to sleep in preparation for morning patrol. 8 paramedics went to sleep in preparation for the morning shift. None of them saw past 10:00 am Sept 11, 2001. In one single moment life may never be the same. As you live and enjoy the breaths you take today and tonight before you go to sleep in preparation for your life tomorrow, kiss the ones you love, snuggle a little tighter, and never take one second of your life for granted."

Unknown

INTRODUCTION

"The attack took place on American soil, but it was an attack on the heart and soul of the civilized world. And the world has come together to fight a new and different war, the first, and we hope the only one, of the 21st century. A war against all those who seek to export terror, and a war against those governments that support or shelter them."

-President George W. Bush, 10/11/01

Tuesday, September 11, 2001, will forever be etched in my heart. I will never forget where I was when I heard the news of the first airplane crashing into the World Trade Center. I'd just dropped my three children off at school and decided to stop at the Kroger Grocery Store on Cascade Road in Atlanta, Georgia when I heard over the loudspeaker, news of an airplane crashing into the World Trade Center. My first thought was...did I hear that right? I begin to notice the people around me stop, as if frozen in place. Before I could react or ask a question, another announcement came that a second airplane had just crashed into the other side of the Trade Center. I was in disbelief, then fear set in.

I left my items on the register and headed back to the school to get my children out. They were confused but I tried to keep my cool because I didn't want to scare them. I didn't tell them anything about the plane crash until we got home. We sat together in front of the television for hours and watched the news repeat the story of the airplanes crashing. Through my own uncertainty, I did what I could to answer their questions and calm their fears.

My children were 11, 9, and 7 years old at that time and I was their only source of comfort. I was the security they depended on to keep them safe. I remember fighting back the tears while trying to explain to them that they were okay, even when the world was still trying to figure out what was happening and not even sure if "we", the United States were okay. No one knew at that time if there were other attacks planned in other parts of the country.

When the dust settled, four airplanes were hijacked by a terrorist extremist group associated with Al Qaeda. Two of the airplanes were flown into the twin towers of the World Trade Center in New York City, a third plane hit the Pentagon just outside Washington, D.C., and the fourth plane crashed in a field in Shanksville, Pennsylvania. Nearly 3000 people were killed, and more than 6000 were injured. The 9/11 attacks on the United States, were the deadliest act of terrorist in the history of the world. After the terrorist attacks of September 11, 2001, President George W. Bush, announced a Global war on Terrorism.

Suited for Service is an anthology of stories from the men and women of the brotherhood who sacrificed their lives for this country. This book is in memory of all those who lost their lives in the pursuit of our civil liberties.

LaQuita Parks

Owner/Publisher: Pa-Pro-Vi

CHAPTER 1 A SOLDIERS STORY
Vaughn Ward

I believe few people in this world find their purpose for being here. Whether a missed chance or a business venture not taken, it all seems to revolve around fear. Fear of moving on, fear of leaving something behind, fear of being alone, fear of failure. But for those that do take those chances and overcome that fear, the world becomes an endless place of wonder.

On June 16th, 2005, I found my purpose as a fresh recruit in the United States Army. With the promise of adventure and to see the world and guaranteed an opportunity to fight for my country, I signed on the dotted line. Up to this point, I had never been on an airplane, I'd never been hundreds of miles away from home, and I had never indeed been on my own. The anticipation and fear swelled up inside, only taking a backseat to the excitement I felt of starting training.

As I entered the Military Entrance Processing Station, I remember seeing all the other recruits given sad goodbyes as tears rolled down their faces. Freckly and pimple-faced teenagers gave away their final hugs and kisses as they were released to the sergeant on duty. We were assigned rooms and told when the wake-up call would be and the form of transportation we were to take in the morning. Some had an eight to twelve-hour bus ride depending on where they would do their initial training. Others had a plane ride to their final destination. Some would be a combo of both.

The thing that separated this batch of recruits from recruits five to six years ago is that we were actively at war. We were guaranteed to see the desert and all of its sandy glory. You could hear all the badasses who couldn't wait to kill some Al-Qaeda, some who had brothers or sisters already in the war. But I don't think any of us were truly prepared for what was to come. Some would go out to celebrate their last few moments of freedom. I enjoyed a good burger and a soda, something I knew I wouldn't see again for a long time. The thing about serving your country is that it is all under contract; they control how you are dressed, when you eat and what you eat. So I wanted all the junk my body could handle in eight hours.

I could barely sleep the night before because, like most, I heard all the horror stories of basic training. I wasn't prepared for the disrespect that would come along with it. Finally, the morning came, and the airplane ride would come; I could feel my stomach touching my back as the plane took off, mixed with a little bit of vomit that I quickly washed down with doubt.

What the hell was I thinking? It is too late to go back now, I thought to myself, all you can do is tough it out. You're strong enough to face anything, trying to psych myself out. Then the calm came, just like the calm before the storm. My body went completely numb, and all my fears just faded to the background as I passed out on the plane ride. I would wake up at Chicago O'Hare Airport, only to run into another gaggle of recruits waiting on the next plane ride. We would fly to Atlanta, Georgia, where we would take a bus to Columbia, South Carolina, Ft. Jackson was the end of the road for me. In the back of my mind, I was thinking it took me thirteen hours to arrive in a state that was about an 8-hour car ride from my hometown in Cincinnati, OH. Something I would soon find out the Army is big on for transportation cheap, not practical.

As we all road on this Bluebird bus, it was utterly silent; not one word was spoken as we arrived in the middle of the night to a bunch of Drill Sergeants yelling at us and corralling us into this building like livestock. Names were yelled out, and lines were formed, and with barely little time to understand what was going on, you were stripped, searched, bald, and dressed in unfamiliar clothes. Honestly, it is impressive how fast they thoroughly whip away your former existence and turn you into someone you barely recognize.

The funny thing about the Army is that everyone is treated the same regardless of background. No offensive tattoos or inappropriate attire is allowed. Still, it doesn't completely change a person's background or how they were raised. I ran into a guy that said he had never seen a black person in the flesh, only on T.V. Which blew my mind. I met a black guy that had never been around so many white people in his life. A Native American that never left the reservation, a former skinhead whose brother had died in the war already, and he just wanted to kill the terrorist.

You take all these personalities and throw them in a group together, and now they are your roomies. You will be closer to these men than you will be with your own family. You are expected to trust and believe that these men will die for you and you for them if that time ever came. This is your new Brotherhood, one that will be built with blood, sweat, and tears.

You quickly found out who the posers were and who were used to being on their own. I had never seen so many grown men crying on the first telephone call home. "Mommy, I miss you," "mom, can you come to get me," "mom, I need you to tell them I don't want to do this, come get me" meanwhile, in the background, the drill sergeants are laughing saying "your ass belongs to me," "mommy can't save you now." It's how you learned not to say anything embarrassing aloud because they would use it as fuel against you later.

When chow time came around, it wasn't a vast selection. It was whatever mystery meat, vegetable, and starch they put on your plate. You ate while moving and never actually sat; you moved in a line the length of a lunch table, and if you hadn't finished eating, all your food just went in the trash, and you just starved until your next meal.

Again this went for everyone; black, white, brown, or yellow, it was equal treatment for all. The military is a great equalizer. Some will sink, and some will swim. It doesn't take long before you are in a routine. It's forced on you—early mornings of physical training, followed by breakfast and more physical training and some classes. Then occasionally, you get a mail call and a chance to make some phone calls home and talk to loved ones. But at night, for just a few hours, your time is your own, we would often sit and talk about what we would do when we got out of training, sometimes we laughed, sometimes we fought, we snuck and played dumb games.

We trained in the rain, sun, cold, tired, sleepy, and exhausted. We stood side by side with one another in some of the harshest conditions, and one thing was constant that war was coming, and according to the drill sergeant, one out of every three of us was sure to die. But, hard work, dedication, and commitment to each other would be the key to our survival.

We were able to push past all biases and differences even if we didn't like one another. We endured all the verbal abuse from the drill sergeants and tough love given. We fought through the mud and came out the other side soldiers. We were brothers in arms dedicated to the Constitution of the United States and each other.

Through the years, I have had the pleasure of working with hundreds of brave men and women, and it has been a privilege and honor to have served with all, but I would like to mention a few whose light was put out way too soon and may they rest in peace until we meet again in Valhalla.

Julian Colvin
Matthew Gallagher
Jordan Bear
Tyler Latta

And to all the others, you will be missed.

I'm the oldest son to Barbarah Edwards and Henry Evans, I was born in Cincinnati OH on May 7th, 1987. I joined the military immediately following High School. I've been married for 8 years to my wife Leann Nicole Ward. We have 3 beautiful kids together. My wife is also a servicemember and a College Graduate with a degree in Healthcare Administration a registered LPN, CNA. I have an Associate Degree from University of Cincinnati in Criminal Justice. I have several Combat tours to Afghanistan and now serve as a Special Forces "Green Beret."

CHAPTER 2 MY HERO
Janet Douglas

Where are you from? Ask any military brat that question and watch the hesitation before answering. I was born in San Francisco, California to what I refer to as "Oklahoma Stock". A US Navy Electronics Technician CPO who spent most of his career stationed on Destroyers in the Pacific Ocean and a former switchboard operator for a telephone company, turned stay at home mom.

My mother had five children: one half-sister (a love child) was nine years my senior and one half-sister six years my junior (conceived from a need for love), and my two brothers, one older and one younger with me, the middle child. My father was a practicing, suffering, high functioning alcoholic and my mom survived in any way she could (valium, socializing, working, hiding) separating herself from her unfavorable situation. Moving from place to place, school to school, making new friends, leaving those friends, change was and still is my lifestyle and I love it!

My father retired and relocated back to Oklahoma when I was 11. Shortly thereafter my parents divorced; my father threw himself into Alcoholics Anonymous, Weight Watchers and the integration into a "Civilian" lifestyle. My mother began her healing journey of finding herself after the tumultuous relationship. My oldest sister had married and stayed in Hawaii leaving me feeling somewhat abandoned since she practically raised me.

I found it difficult to adjust to the slower, more family oriented, locationally planted, bible belt population that was Oklahoma. My accent and awkwardness left me feeling like the outsider that I was. At sixteen, with an above average intelligence, a worldly upbringing, raging hormones, and little to no parental guidance, I solved my seemingly impossible task of filling into society with drugs and alcohol.

In a matter of months, I went from an honor roll student, pep club, French club, Chemistry teacher's aide.... To manager of a recreation game room where I provided smokes, drugs, and alcohol to minors like me who were bored with school and life; we had all the answers. As a minor, I also provided the solution to major players in the distribution of illegal substances.

My senior year, needing only four classes for one semester to graduate, I carried a B average although attending less than half of the days required. When I was finally led into the councilor's office, they informed me that I had failed due to absences, and we reconstructed my future schedule to entice me into completing my education. I had applied, and was hired, to work for Southwestern Bell, earning a higher salary at 17 than my mother was at 46 although shortly after she did rehire and retire. I dropped out of school and entered in the workforce with all its rules and regulations.

Consistent with my need for change, less than 6 months passed when I woke up with an awful hangover, in an obscure place, with incredibly unique people and as I looked around, I knew this was not the future I envisioned. I went home, quit my job, and requested of my older sister, then residing in California, to make the move and a fresh start with her. She agreed. Little did I know I was walking from the fire into the oven. Her then boyfriend fed me drugs, repeatedly forced himself on me and upon informing my sister, she replied "It's ok, we have an open relationship!"

I could think of only one other solution and since I was always striving to be my father's best son, I joined the US Navy. I needed the Navy; the Navy did not necessarily need me. Best decision I have ever made in my life! The military training and lifestyle were just what I needed to get order and balance back in my life. Clear instructions and direction. Clear hierarchy in the chain of command. Overwhelming sense of belonging and community.

I thrived in Boot Camp. I was not the squad leader, but she was my best friend! I loved organizing the blow dryers, so the cords were smoothly wrapped around the handles, and that every piece of micro trash or speck of dust was eliminated. I coached a few of the older ladies (mid 20's) to complete the required Physical Tests. My father's training me in the art of massage paid off when the ladies had head or muscle aches. My shining personality and smile helped encourage and lift the spirits of the stressed ladies in my squadron. I was in my element!

I joined the service as an Airman and I was given orders to Honolulu, Hawaii; however, when the opportunity came up for Fireman School, I grabbed it! I loved getting greasy, so I was thrilled when I was sent to the Naval Facility in Keflavik Iceland to maintain the engines that provided stable power for the pertinent electronics. I was told there was a woman behind every tree and that everyone was avid worshippers. Iceland was all but void of trees, however, Keflavik hosted many churches of different denominations as well as my favorite spirits served by the shot at the Top Of The Rock.

Since my love to serve equaled my love to dance, I took a second job as a waitress. We would often leave work only to continue the party in the barracks and on one occasion after hosting a formal banquet clad in a dress borrowed from my roommate, we went to the room of an Air Force man. I fell in love totally and whole heartedly. We were engaged before daybreak and married within 6 months. He rotated out to, of all places, Oklahoma City, OK. I continued my tour in Iceland for another 4 months and spent 30 days in Oklahoma before heading to Engineman "A" School in Great Lakes, IL. "A" school was a breeze since I had just spent the last year doing 2 major and 4 minor overhauls on the 671 Detroit diesels used to power the Naval Facility.

Again, I thrived personally and professionally. Diversity of people, cultures and locations brings me the ultimate joy! When my friends suggested we go dancing at a club just outside the base, I happily joined even though at nineteen, I was not of legal age to drink alcohol. I remember having a great time dancing, I remember somebody handing me a drink, I remember feeling sick and going outside for air, I remember being forced into a car, I remember moments of waking with someone on top of me, I remember feeling pain and knowing that something was terribly wrong, I remember waking up in a strange bed.

Two men dressed in blues were sitting on the couch; both refused to speak, refused to even look at me, refused to answer my frantic questions. Finally, I asked for a ride back to the base and one said, "Phillip had the duty, he has the only car". There were three. I shuffled out the door full of fear and confusion, physically beaten. I begged for coinage to make a call and was given a quarter so I could make 2 calls. I called my barracks roommate who agreed to meet me with cab fare, and I called a cab.

Lynn was the only person I talked to about what had happened to me. I felt so ashamed, I felt I had done something wrong; I just knew everyone would hate me if they found out, especially my new husband who was 1500 miles away. I was in the Navy, women were in the minority, in 1980 and unlike today, military sexual trauma was pushed under the rug. Men and women were being physically, sexually, and verbally abused; and the environment was "don't talk, don't tell, suck it up and do your job."

Two weeks later I had graduated "A" school, spent another 30 days in Oklahoma with my husband, and headed out to the USS Canopus, a submarine tender docked in Charleston South Carolina. Three weeks after that, a positive pregnancy test, separation from the ship due to possible radiation exposure, and separation from my husband; the decision was made, and I was given an honorable medical discharge. Physically all indications were that my husband was indeed the father of our daughter. The slim possibility otherwise was unthinkable, and I carried that secret, one I thought I would take to the grave with me, for the next 35 years.

Although I did my best to maintain a healthy outlook on life, I had changed. Fear of repeated circumstance and abandonment, self-doubt and self-loathing caused deep depression and anxiety and although I was able to maintain the relationship long enough to birth our second daughter, we agreed to end the 7-year marriage. Their father was a family oriented, loving man and in my state of mind, the greatest act of love I could do for my girls was to allow him full custody. Another reason to be shunned from society and judged by self and others as incompetent.

Traveling was in my blood and running from my problems seemed to help with the feelings of worthlessness, so I fulfilled my childhood dream of becoming an Over the Road Truck Driver. The lifestyle suited me for several years and once feeling healthy enough to enter the "real world", I took on a local driving job; eventually hiring on with the intermodal operations of the Santa Fe Railroad. I was successfully rising in the ranks despite the depression and found out that if I indulged myself at night in alcohol, I could maintain a pleasant productive attitude at work.

My first born was having trouble adjusting to the restrictions and personalities of her dad and stepmother so at the age of 11, she was granted permission to come live with me. My second born continued to live with her father, visiting us every summer and communicating by phone frequently. I married again, not for love, he had great health insurance and a son that lived with him. As well as four additional children and five ex-wives. He lived in a tent in his mom's back yard after being kicked out from the last baby-momma but I could fix all that and I was desperate to give his son a real mom.

The physical abuse began five days after the

wedding and I stayed anyway, his son needed me, and if I could just be the perfect wife and mother he would change. When his son hit my daughter, I left. Although the marriage lasted less than a year, the divorce settlement took another two years (I had money and he wanted it) during which I moved to Texas to avoid his stalking, graffiti, and constant damage to my property.

From the ashes rose the Phoenix again and although a high functioning alcoholic now, I thrived in Texas transforming from employee to mid-level management and eventually was given my own terminal. I was a startup queen in a king's world. Our company would obtain new contracts for the intermodal facilities; I would implement them from start to finish which included the pencil used to fill out the applications, hiring/training employees, all purchasing/leasing of equipment, creation, and implementation of policies/procedures, and overseeing the first few weeks to ensure all transitioned smoothly.

Personally, the drugs, alcohol, and plethora of men, allowed me to escape the pain and loneliness that self-hate brings. The occasional trip to the psychiatrist only left an endless trial/error of medications that would allow me to alleviate the symptoms of depression while allowing me to function at the high level necessary to maintain my position within the company. Therapy was not my forte; one doctor fell asleep while I was talking.

Although thriving in school, my daughter was party to the same cycle of one alcoholic parent and one that was unavailable both physically and mentally. Upon graduating high school, she continued the path I had help set her on of drugs, alcohol, and men. We did not speak again for almost 2 years; she had become pregnant and needed help. Moving her and her boyfriend to Houston with me, providing them housing and vehicles proved to be too little too late. With one little decision my world turned upside down again.

After everything I had done for her and everything, he had done to her, she still chose to move in with her father in California. I was devastated, I wasn't even good enough to be a grandparent. With more self-loathing and feelings of worthlessness as a human being, my alcohol consumption rose to new heights.

I had always thought that I would not live to see 40. When I quit drinking and entered the world of Alcoholics Anonymous, my old life did die in a way. Without the alcohol my mind exploded in thousands of thoughts, never ending, gifts of the spirit were overwhelming. I could no longer play the mind games that I thought were required of me to be successful in a "man's" world. I had to speak my truth and I could only cope in an either/or world; grey was not an option. I cashed out my 401K.

My company and I mutually agreed that I would no longer be under their employ. With a hefty severance pay and no contest to unemployment benefits, I set off to help others. At the end of 9 months, I had an unbirthed non-profit company, a sailboat, and a limited cell phone plan. I still owed thousands on my credit cards and on my 6-year-old pickup. I moved into the sailboat, started selling bait for the marina, began drinking, and vowed never to be a quitter again.

The alcohol quieted the mind and left me

focused and productive. I began with doing the Marina's bookkeeping and ended up as the Harbor Master's assistant and manager of the Icehouse. Drinking was almost encouraged and other than the Harbor Master himself, all the employees indulged to various degrees. In the aftermath of hurricane Katrina in New Orleans LA, hurricane Rita demolished my marina and since I lived in the bay house, I lost everything, my home, my boat, and my job. My second daughter requested my presence in Maine since she and her husband were about to start a family of their own and she was wanting to get to know her mother better.

Even after landing a great bookkeeping job and moving into my own apartment, the depression, anxiety, panic attacks and alcoholism, led me to attempting a permanent solution to my temporary problem. I spent thirty-six hours trying not to be here today. After the hospitalization, psychological institution, and alcohol rehabilitation center I made another life changing decision. If God was not going to allow me to die, then I refuse to live like I had over the last thirty years.

I began a healing journey which included the help of my family and friends, both medical and psychological professionals, conventional, holistic, and spiritual approaches, self-help books, life coaches, as well as becoming vulnerable within Veteran groups. Early in this journey, I found that I was eligible for Veteran benefits which opened exponentially the resources for my wellbeing both physically and mentally. I was given excellent individual and group care through the Veteran's Administration Medical and Mental health programs. In my experience, the community outreach for Veterans is tremendous and today I receive top notch treatment from military and civilian population.

My daughter's questionable paternity? After many years of spending time with other veterans that had experienced military sexual trauma, I found a safe place to unburden my heart and speak my truth out loud. The younger one I told first, she is my rock and foundation. She keeps me grounded and tells me in no uncertain terms her opinions and recommendations. She agreed to take a DNA test that would determine whether or not they were full siblings. Armed with the tests and an apprehensive heart, I flew to California and explained the situation. Seemed almost a relief when she heard; she had always thought of herself as an Alien.

The DNA results revealed she was of this world; however, not of her believed to be father. She was conceived in violence and that knowledge sent her down an unknown path which she walks today with Curiosity, Grace, and Gratitude. Her father was, as you can imagine, devastated, and yet assured her that his love for her was strong and true as it ever was. Feeling a bit selfish, needing self-healing, caused much pain in many people and to this day my goal is to live each day with the intention to bring only joy to others, never hurt or pain.

They say it takes a village to raise a child and I agree. The last 13 years I have used the world and all its resources to overcome my past and learn the answer to the one of the most difficult questions one can ask yourself... Who Am I? This quest will be a lifelong search, one that I look forward to with excitement each revelation. I now wake every morning stating 5 things to be grateful. I strive to think, speak, and act with appreciation, compassion, understanding, forgiveness, humility, and valor. I am my own hero and I continue to strengthen my connection to spirit and honor the gifts freely given to me.

Today, if I use the tools and resources available, I maintain a healthy mind, body, and soul. I live an abundant life, traveling around the United States using my regained sparkling personality and social media to help others see their self-worth, heal their wounds, and help me in my mission to "Heal the world, One smile at a time!"

 Janet L. Douglas, Navy veteran and mother of 2 travels the world helping others to overcome their past, roadblocks and limiting beliefs. As a spiritual healer, a recovering alcoholic and a universal connector, Janet bridges the gap and provides solutions, information, and contacts for all those who cross her path with the challenges they face.

Janet is an author, speaker and infopreneur committed to informing the citizens of the world (nomads) how to live their best life. She teaches others how to manifest abundance thru receiving and sharing information and she is willing to teach you, too.

Janet works remotely on several digital platforms allowing her the financial freedom to live and travel as she chooses. Janet is open to all collaborations with those who host public or private media outlets or events including podcasts, YouTube, bootcamps, master classes etc.

Reach out to Janet via Facebook, ClubHouse, Instagram (iMoonshot) etc.

_T_

CHAPTER 3 THE HEARTBEATS NO ONE SEES
David Patterson

Being a solider can be challenging, unpredictable, and rewarding, making certain moments a breath-taking experience. Many times, people will come up to a soldier with a sense of pride, compassion, and love that flows with respect, especially if you are in your uniform. There just seems to be something about an individual in a uniform that captures the attention of people. It's funny though. These virtues are not based on whether you are a good or bad solider, just the fact that you are a solider, can earn you recognition within that moment of one's encounter.

I know this to be true because I served thirty-seven years of my life wearing the uniform with pride and dignity, and I never wanted to retire from the Armed Forces because I loved it with all my heart. I heard it said that 'when you love what you do, it's not work," and trust me for the most part it was just a love that embraced my heart tightly; like a vice grip that at times caused emotional pain but pain that also hurt so good.

My career took me places that a poor boy from Detroit would have never seen, gave me experiences that many will only see on their big screen or read in a book. I had adventures that I saw in the National Geographics, and pleasures that you would only read in a romance novel or travel magazines of exotic places that one wished they could enjoy and embrace.

I met people that had rank, status and positions that allowed them to be seen and live like Rock Stars and those who were so poor, that you would just describe them as "po." Yet in all that, I was able to gather knowledge, wisdom, and understanding of the heart of man and the spirit of a solider.

Each person I have met directly or indirectly, I believe was a walking book filled with many chapters, which if given the opportunity to meet and read them, you would gain a wealth of knowledge about the nature of our human experience. Therefore, exposing me to the various levels of people's true selves, without being that individual. Now without sounding pretentious, I believe my ability to read individual books allowed me to understand the real nature of the person. I believe this was due to my beautiful parents and grandparents who taught me the importance of developing people skills, and this was especially true about my grandfather who was a solider himself.

This teaching allowed me to go anywhere in the world as an African American man, as well as a soldier, building working and emotional relationships that would permit me to read several chapters from any individual book. Everyone had a story to tell from civilians to my fellow soldiers across the globe.

My experiences have permitted me to experience the cold winters of Germany and their iconic Castles, to the Southeast Asia country of Thailand with its stunning Islands and beaches.

Then moving into the unbearable heat and sandstorms of Iraq and snow cap mountains of Afghanistan. Either way, each experience enhanced my knowledge of us as human beings. Whether it was the knowledge of the culture, ethnicity, traditions, or how we deal with uncomfortable challenges, emotionally, psychologically, and intellectually, it all brought me to one conclusion: We as a people experience the depth of life's problems and challenges in similar manners even though our environment, cultural styles and lifestyles may change, many of the problems pretty much remain the same. We all have core issues of life that we live with, which can range from relational, financial, emotional, psychological, and physical. Different people, different presentations, but still a centralized theme exists; we are all just huma beings trying to figure out this thing called life.

This leads me right into what I found to be within the Spirit of a solider which taps right into the heartbeat that many can't or won't see, but another soldier will. There is something unique that is deep rooted inside the Spirit of a solider for which only another soldier can identify with, and even more so a solider that has experienced war. This thought even takes that soldiers spirit to another plane for which not even the non-war veteran can understand.

As I reminisce, about being deployed to Iraq in 2003 and coming home in 2005, many thoughts run through my mind. I was deployed with a 785th Combat Stress Control Unit, which was a Behavior Health Unit that assisted soldiers in dealing with the challenges that could have a life changing impact on a soldier's life that will live with them for a lifetime.

You see, I personally have held many roles in the United States Army, but this one was different because it allowed me to go into the world of the soldiers that no one got to know. This is the world, which everyone on the civilian side of the house finds hard to understand and can be totally misinterpreted even when the professionals try to address-the outcome.

This world is private and hard to enter unless you are a soldier who has been there, not by way of vicarious understanding but directly impacted by the smell, the sounds, the scream, the pain, the hurt and the losses that a war veteran lives through, if they even live. However, under the Blackjack Brigade leadership, our brigade's Operation Iraqi Freedom I/II 14-month deployment Blackjack soldiers saw action in Western Baghdad, Najaf, Fallujah, and Northern Babel.

This would test the very spirit of any solider. No one was exempt from the hard realities of war. All too often for me, the spirit of annoyance rises up when I watch movies and TV and see actors playing soldiers but not signing up to be one. This observation turns my stomach, because of those people who portray being a solider, yet don't understand the harsh realities that we face.

However, the events that take place during April 2004 called Black Sunday would impact our lives forever and a day! For the sake of privacy, I won't expand on the details of the events, but I will say the aftermath changed our lives forever. I've experienced countless soldiers and families, including my own who are suffering from brain diseases and physical injuries who are all left with the remnants of its effects.

Especially when you consider what we call the unseen wounds that don't heal, such as Post

Traumatic Stress Disorder, (PTSD) and Traumatic Brain Injury (TBI). It's not uncommon to hear civilians call their Uncle John crazy or make statements about the brother or sister that's seen on the street, who may have a sign in their hand saying will "work for food as you pass them by. People make statements like "they should get a job." Or the classic statement, I've heard people say, "Why don't they go get help? the Veterans Administration can get help for them." Truthfully most people have no real clue to the challenges that a veteran face attempting to navigate through the bureaucracy of the VA's red tape; that can leave a halfway healthy veteran exhausted. Let alone the veteran who have been ravished with mental and emotional and the obvious physical challenges to deal with after a stint in the war zone of any campaign.

I have heard people in my circle make comments such as, "My friend said, he can get benefits, or all veterans got benefits, just go down to the VA, because my friend got his benefits." These statements and more are so narrow in perspective and understanding because of the lack of knowledge that people have about a soldier's story, it leaves veterans angry, frustrated, irritated, and segregated, which for many veterans just don't even want the headache and hassles of even dealing with society, family or as mentioned the Veteran Administrations disrespectful insensitive nonsense.

Many solider can't speak about the challenges they have faced because people just don't understand. One of my fellow soldiers, whose name I will keep anonymous, put it this way, "After I returned from my first deployment, when asked what I did in the war zone, I said that I composed and fused bombs ranging from Laser guided bombs, Satellite guided bombs, Miniature bombs, enormous bombs or very special bombs. In the event that it detonates, I more than likely put it together."

In any case, I immediately discovered that answer normally slaughtered the discussion - it even finished a couple of first dates early. It was something abnormal to rise up in everyday discussions. I in the end figured out how to be dubious and say something vague. Generally they wouldn't pose additional inquiries.

I don't regularly discuss what I did, or precisely how I feel about it. What's more, in truth, I feel conflicted. I realize that occasionally I helped save American lives by managing my work competently. Our guys. My friends. And that makes me proud. But that doesn't change the fact that I contributed - however indirectly to human beings vanishing from the earth in a moment of sheer agony." You see the Spirit of a solider goes beyond the visible, of just dawning a uniform, doing a service, being a part of the few, proud and the brave; it's more about the challenges we face when the war is over, when the uniform is removed, and the ban of brothers and sisters are no longer around.

The bullets stop, the sound of the bombs is no more, the yelling and screaming ends and you are no longer a part of a family that is there with you until the end. You now are alone left with the spirit of being a solider, who has seen more in a short block of time, than many will see in a lifetime. You are left with your own devices to defend for yourself. You were trained to kill or be killed; you were conditioned to live in the moment and not one moment over.

You were trained to survive and to complete the mission, but you were never trained to turn it off.

The Spirit of the soldier is now left to deal with the wounds that don't bleed, in the wilderness known as civilian life, where the Devil has now opened his door to hell and there's no angel to minister or save you. It's just the Spirit of a solider that's left within, to defend for them. Even when the solider is presented with illusions of concern, support, and resources, only for the solider to find out that it wasn't authentic but a carbon copy, a fake document to create the idea to the world that there is support for veterans and all they have to do is seek help.

Yet like the devil, when you thought he really cared, you find out, he was just a wolf in sheep's clothing pretending to be gentle and kind but in truth, it was a slide of the hand that tricked the solider, that devastated their spirit, heart, and mind. However, there's always a silver lining when God is involved, for He comes and touches the heart of a solider by giving him or her a clean heart and renewing the right spirit in them.

As God's word say's in Psalm 51: 10 "Create in me a clean heart, O God; renew a right spirit within me." For the soldiers who I have worked with and shared many long hours of conversation, their saving grace is accepting Christ as their personal Lord and Savior.

I have found that this has led many lonely and heartbroken soldiers away from the life of depression, anxiety, suicide, and homicidal thoughts that could have destroyed their lives. I personally have lost seven out of ten in my own PTSD group to this device of Satan. Accepting Christ has helped us remaining soldier's work on the issues that plague our minds, our hearts, and our spirits. Saving us from our guilt of not being the people we were before we went to war, which has impacted our relationships with our spouses, children, friends, jobs, and a host of other relationships, because we are misunderstood by ourselves and others. With the help of God, we will come out of the wilderness of despair and be comforted by the Holy Spirit to truly be God's image bearer that represents the spirit of a soldier.

David Patterson is on a mission to be a change agent in the world of the youth. With 37 years of military experience, he has trained hundreds of soldiers throughout his career. Trained in the area of counseling, fitness, resiliency, and leadership, and formally educated in all three domains. He has developed a strong foundation in communication, motivation and inspiration that has inspired others to maximize on their God given potential. With a high level of commitment to bringing diversity into the youth forethought, teaching the youth to not be a time consumer but a future producer. Emphasizing Education, Self-development, Community and Spiritual connection, he sees a future transition of the youth, working in harmony and changing the world one individual at a time.

J

CHAPTER 4 THE FIRST PART OF THE JOURNEY
Gwen Marshall

It was 1976. Can you picture a 19-year-old girl that has never been away from home, who is already married and has one child. Who literally moved out of the house with her Father and in with a husband who is also a 19-year-old boy? We couldn't really afford college, so my two bother-in-laws, and my husband's best friend had all joined the military, and so why not I. We are going to go to the Military. My God Mother said that she would keep our daughter until we got out of basic training, so off to the recruiter we went.

I must admit looking back I got a good recruiter. He was very honest with me (I had been told that most were not), however everything he told me is exactly what happened. He started out by asking me what I would like to do. I told him that I loved biology. He suggested the Air Force, so I took his advice and I chose the Air Force. I selected Environmental Health Specialist as my Career Path. He told me that I would have to take the entry exam which would be the determining factor on whether or not I would in fact be able to do what I had chosen, and it would also determine if I would be able to choose the Air Force as my branch of the service. If not, I would have to go into another branch of the service, as well as choose another career path. He made an appointment for the both of us to take the test.

Test time came, and I went in there and gave it my best shot. My recruiter called a few days later to tell us that the test results came back, so we went into the recruiting office see him. He kept me in a bit of suspense. I was so nervous. I wanted to know how I had done; the suspense was killing me. I was a little girl. Green with no world experience, and all this was so unfamiliar to me. I was so scared, but in some ways, I wasn't scared at all. I felt like I could make this work, yet I was still unsure. It was all new to me. Drumroll please... I passed with flying colors. I was in the top 90% Wow!!! Of course, I was happy, excited, and scared all at the same time. I could do exactly what I wanted to do. It was a dream come true or was it?

Well, my husband decided not to go. He didn't do as well on the test as I did, so he would not be able to enter the Air Force. He would have to go into the Army, and there was no guarantee that we would be able to get stationed close to each other. In fact, there was not any guarantee that we would even be in the same state. They said they would do the best they could, however there was no guarantee. So, at the last minute he decided he did not want to go. He was not going to enter the Military at all. So now I was on my own. I was going to have to go this alone. I decided that I was going to see it through, I was not going to back out. I scheduled my swearing in for two weeks out. It gave me time to get myself, my daughter, and my husband together before I left. I was off on this new journey.

That two weeks passed very quickly, so now it is time to leave. Time to say my "Goodbyes". My husband takes me to my swearing in. My stomach is full of knots. I look at him with teary eyes, and we both now have teary eyes. He asked did I want to change my mind. I said "No" I am going to do it. I am going to do what I said I was going to do. I did not want to leave him, nor did I want to leave my baby daughter, but this was a chance to make a better life, and I wanted to do exactly what I said that I would do. It was not war time, so I wasn't going off to war. I dried my eyes, and I swore in, I got on the plane, and I left for Basic Training in San Antonio, Texas.

After a three-hour plane ride, and another short bus ride I am at Lackland Air Force Base in San Antonio, Texas. Now when we left San Francisco we all rode together. Which means that the girls and guys rode together. When we got to the airport in San Antonio, Texas they split us up before we got on the bus. The guys rode one bus, and the girls rode another. I got off the bus to loud voices. They were almost screaming. It was the drill sergeants coming to greet us in their own special way. I start to wonder did I make the right choice. Keep in mind that I grew up in the house with a father that almost never raised his voice above a whisper. Not even when he was angry.

Now they had already assigned you to a Drill Sergeant, so when you got off the bus, they called you by name. We lined up, and the intimidation began. They began to tell you that you belonged to the United States Air Force. Your parents nor anyone else could save you. You will follow the rules, and you will do as you are told. I was standing there trying to look at some of the faces of the other young women. Not easy to do since you must look straight ahead. All I was able to do was look out of the corner of my eyes. What I saw was the look of fear. I could only imagine that this had to be new for them as well. We were all scared. We were all terrified. I know I was.

Now this was during a time when there was no such thing as a cell phone. Landlines and phone booths were what we were working with, and if you know anything about the Military you could not call home during basic training. Basic training was six weeks. and I would only be able to use the phone the last week of basic. The only way I could keep in touch with my family was by writing a letter. A good old fashion letter. I wrote them all every week. I wrote, even if I didn't have much to say.

I had never been away from my father, even though I was married I still saw my dad almost every single day. I couldn't see my daughter, my husband, my friends, no one. No one other than the other young women in my squad. I was as they say really "green" a true fish out of water. My plan was to fake it until I make it. Those were young women that I did not know, and they did not know me. We were all there for the same reason "to change our lives". Or so we thought.

The first couple of weeks it was new, exciting, and scary all together. Lots to learn. My Drill Sergeant seemed to be okay for the most part. She was very petite, but what I really meant is that she was short. Short and muscular and had short blonde hair. She was a Master Sergeant. She never smiled, and she did a lot of yelling. Since my Recruiter had informed me that this would be the norm, I was not surprised. I didn't expect it, but then again, I didn't know quite what to expect. From the bus they took you to the barracks where you would stay and allowed you to put your things away. It wasn't much since you were not allowed to take much with you, and there really wasn't a reason to take it anyway.

Most of our day consisted of drills and exercise. We could mingle among ourselves until "lights out". This meant it was time for bed. No, you didn't get to go to bed when you felt like it, you went to bed when they told you to. We got up the next morning and went to the chow hall for breakfast, then to the clinic. Everyone was required to get shots. We were kept in close quarters, and since they really had no way to know whether everyone was up to date on their shots, everyone got them. Then we got our basic training uniforms. Those uniforms separated you from everyone else on base. Everyone was wearing a uniform, but those uniforms let everyone know that you were a rookie, you were new, and you were green.

You got pants, shirts, dress hat, baseball cap, jacket, sweater, and socks and shoes. They were standard issue and that is exactly how they fit. Just like standard issue. They just hang. Not fitted at all. Everyone looked the same, the only thing different was the face and hair. Next, we were off to the barbershop. It was worked out so that one troop comes in and the other is going out. The girls were coming in and the guys were coming out. Military does not allow real long hair. The barbers and beauticians were lined up each with a chair, and those that must get a cut will get a cut. It was not negotiable.

For men, I think it is not more than an inch and a half. For women if it is longer than shoulder length you must be able to get your hat on properly with your hair rolled up in a bun. If you wore an afro, you were required to be able to put on your hat properly, and it must ft properly. I had to do what we called back then "pack it". In other words, I had to wet it and pat it down, so that I could get it on. After a few tries, I found someone in the group that could French braid hair. I French braid as well, so the skill came in handy. I saw lots of guys get their hair cut, and I do mean they left piles of hair on the floor. Quite a few of the girls ended up having to cut theirs as well.

Somewhere in between all of this we went to lunch, and now it was about time for dinner or "chow" as it is called. We were getting set up for the hammer to drop. We had no idea what was about to come. So far it seemed pretty good. We got back to the barracks, mixed and mingled amongst ourselves, and lights out. During the mix and mingle everyone was trying on their uniforms making sure that everything fit. Basically, they asked you your size, and that is what they handed you, or a size larger. Never too tight. We had gotten our shots, haircuts, uniforms, and now that was when it started to change.

The military was designed to build teamwork. We were going to do everything together. When we marched, we marched together, when we ran, we ran together, when we got in trouble, we were going to get in trouble together. They got you up in the dark! Yes 4am or 5am every morning. You got up to the lights coming on and the loud noise. "Let's Go Ladies! You got up, and you had a limited amount of time to get dressed, so if you were a makeup girl, there would be no makeup. Now everyone got dressed together. Yes, no doors on the showers, no private stalls, so everybody got to see everybody else. No point in being ashamed or embarrassed since the last thing you wanted to do was be late or be the last person to get into formation. If you were the last person you were going to be called out, and the rest of the squad may have to do extra jumping jacks, or lose some free time, because you messed up. We were a team, so everyone paid for your mistake.

You can only imagine that did not go over well with the rest of the squad. You could become unliked, and very quickly. You had to be in this squad, it was chosen for you. What I learned was that it really doesn't matter what you thought of another team member the idea was to figure out how to get along. How to be the best that you could be together. I think that's where so many people go wrong today. They think that everything is about them, and them only.

They also taught you how to make up a bed. Make up a military bed (which is what we would call a cot). I don't think it was large as a twin-size bed. That bed had to be made up so tight you could bounce a nickel on it. Yes, a nickel and it did have to bounce, and yes, she did check your bed! If you were smart you would check it too. Before she got there. It took a bit of practice and it was not easy at all. It didn't take me long since I wanted to do my best. I was always taught that whatever you do, do it well. I would be practicing when others were sitting around (during their free time).

Now you got some small perks for doing a very good job. Maybe you got to break from squad a little early, or you got to be first in the chow line. Something everyone did not get to do. This was for taking pride in what you did. It emphasized something that my father had taught me "Whatever you do, do it well". Try to always do whatever you do, do it in excellence. I began to strive for excellence. I got so good I began to help some of the others with their cots. I began to teach them how to get it done. So they too could get perks for good performance.

Basic Training to me was a character builder. It was a lot of physical fitness, and toward the end there would be a little competition. Around the third week in things started to change. People started to leave. They used every excuse they could find. Sergeant started to get tough, she had less patience for mistakes. Rightly so, we did the same things all the time, so you would think that practice would make perfect. However, only the strong will survive! Drug abuse, medical reasons, you name it, if you could use it to go home, they used it. We started with a full squad, and gradually they fell of one, by one. My recruiter told me before I left that Boot Camp was a mental journey, and if I could just play the game, I would survive it. I would be alright. It was just a means to the end. The end was a new journey, a new opportunity, so I played along. For me it was a means to an education. One that I am using to this day.

The first time she got up in my face and raised her voice at me I remembered what'd he told me. I looked her right in the eye, and I didn't blink. I didn't move. I answered her in the appropriate manner, and she never did it again. I don't know what my eyes told her, because I don't even know what I was thinking. I was so scared; I couldn't tell you if I wanted to. I was really scared, however somehow, I managed to not let her know that, because the others that let her know they were scared she always managed to find something to yell at them for.

I guess she said there was no point in doing it to me, because I was not going to break. I was not going to show fear. "Never show fear." My reward was

that she would make me a "Squad Leader". Yes, she
made me a Squad Leader! Now that's a top honor in
Boot Camp! It doesn't get much better than that.
They break you up into 4 Squads within the whole
squad, and you are responsible for your squad.
Everybody in your squad sleeps on your row of bunks.
Remember I did not get to pick my squad, so I had to
work with what I had. It doesn't matter, you make
what you have work. You find a way. Real life. I lead
my squad and I led them well.

I had a bit of an advantage since I was probably
one of the only people there that had been on a drill
team, and previously been the leader of a drill team.
We had one at my church. We were good. We
performed in the local parades around town. We went
to perform in competition, and we won quite a few.
So, this was all too familiar to me. So, the marching
came easy to me. Keeping step and keeping time that
was not a challenge for me. We marched, and we
marched. I had my squad practice sometime when we
had free time. We came up with some cute chants.
You know those ones you hear in the movies. Yes, one
of those! We tried to make it fun, and soon the other
squad leaders made up one too, so we got a chance to

use them all. When we would march by another squad, they would do theirs and we would do ours. Much like a little friendly competition.

We are more than three weeks in, and by this time I was really missing my family. Many times, I wanted to cry, but I never wanted to quit. I was not going to give up. I was going to see it through. I had written quite a few letters, and I had gotten several back. I was grateful. Some of these young ladies didn't get letters. No one wrote, and no one called when we were able to make or take phone calls. I can only imagine that being hard, however I realized that some people join the military to have a family. Why, because these strangers will become friends, and these friends will become family.

We were getting down to the end of Basic Training. We began to get a little free time, and things got just a little more relaxed and people were getting to know each other better. Some became friends, and some became foes. What I mean by that is that you learned to tolerate some because they were there, and you really did not have a choice. One day we were in the barracks hanging out, and one of the young ladies in my squad had a picture sitting on her bed. I picked up the picture, and she said "Gwen give it to me" I took off on a fast walk, and she was right behind me. I went around to the other side where the other two rows of bunks were, and Sergeant's office was in the middle.

One of the squad leaders on the other side (white). I don't know if she had a problem with black people, or she just had a problem with me. She blocked my path and said, "give it back to her" I said, "mind your own business, we are just playing". We had an exchange of words, and she got in my face. I did the most frustrating thing you can do to someone I Laughed! I laughed in her face. Now I have never been a fighter, however that does not mean I can't nor do it mean I won't. My gut told me I just needed to walk away. That's what I did, I walked away, and we went back on our side.

Now you must know we had someone that would tell Sergeant everything. Yes everything, so if you were smart you avoided doing anything that would get you in trouble. We got up the next morning, and Sergeant came in, she goes into her office as usual. A few minutes later she calls my name. Marshall, report to my office!" I go to her office, and she tells me to come in. I walked in. She starts by saying "So what happened here yesterday when I was gone? I began to tell her. I didn't flinch. I didn't raise my voice. No drama whatsoever. I merely told her that we were kidding around, I grabbed the picture, and fast walked around to the other side, and you know the rest. I told her I gave the picture back, and everything was fine. We had a good laugh about it when we got back around on the other side.

Sergeant dismissed me from her office, and she called the other young lady into her office. After a minute or so we began to hear Sergeant speaking at the top of her lungs. My bunk was first bunk right at Sergeant's office, so I had a decent ear shot. I couldn't really hear the conversation since she had the door closed, however we did hear the fallout. Next thing we know she came out of there in tears, and her face was so red. I had never seen anything like it. Next, Sergeant called me back into her office. She began to tell me that my side of the story had been confirmed, and that I had been doing a great job. She also said that she was proud of the way I handled that situation,

and for that I would not receive any type of
punishment, however she was going to strip the other
young lady of her title as Squad Leader. She asked me
if I had any suggestions. I did give her a couple of
names, and she picked one of them.

The young lady she chose was black, she was
very pretty, had long black hair, and was tall. I cannot
remember her name; however, I have never forgotten
that face. The new formation had begun. We had
already had a few changes, because people had asked
to be discharged, and they had left, however we were
at least a month in the Basic Training now. Change
could happen at the drop of a hat. Things could
change without any notice. She fell right in as if she
had been there all along. You would have never
thought she was a replacement. I had a few people
mad at me since they thought I should have lost my
spot as well, however I didn't. I didn't because it was
not the situation, it was how I handled it. It may have
been what I didn't say as opposed to what I did say...
which was not much. In this case less was more.

The only words Sergeant and I had after that
was when one of the young ladies in the squad

collapsed. We were out marching, and it was hot. It was summer in San Antonio, Texas. If you know anything about Texas weather, you know that is hot and humid. We were standing in formation, and this young lady started to rock front to back. The next thing we know she hit the ground. I mean she fell flat on her face. She fell face first and hit the concrete. She hit the concrete so hard, she bounced. I had never seen anything like it in my life at that time. I could not keep my composure. I began to cry. I could not pull it together.

Sergeant called my name "Marshall". She told me to pull it together. I began to try to pull myself together. I must admit that was hard. It was hard to see that. It still hurts to this day when I think about it. The ambulance was called, and a couple of days later she returned to the barracks. She was banged up pretty bad. The concrete had taken the skin off her cheek. She had hurt her arm. And of course, she was limping. She was excused from any of the other duties for the time being. Everyone welcomed her back, and we never spoke on it again.

The final weeks were there. A little more

relaxed, a little freer time. Now I knew that my husband's best friend was there somewhere. Now he was a dear friend to me as well. We all grew up together, we went to school together. I knew he probably left for basic training only a week or two ahead of me. He was close to leaving. I was hoping that I would run into him somewhere. I was hoping I would see him. He would be a familiar face. It would remind me of home. It would bring me some comfort. Well that day came. I was walking across the quadrant and I heard someone call my name. I knew the voice, and it is him! I stopped to talk. We had to hurry because we were not supposed to talk to each other. It was one of the rules, so we had to make it fast.

Out of nowhere comes Sergeant. Yes, she appeared. I do not remember what she said, but I do remember the look on her face, so we scurried on. I did get a chance to tell him that Ron and my daughter would be there soon. They should arrive a few days before I got out. They might get a chance to see each other, and they did. It would be the last time they saw each other for almost five years.

The time had come, and Basic Training is over. It was time to go. It was time for the next chapter which for me was school, lots of school. I had six weeks of training for my job classification to come, however I did not know where that would be and I would not find out until just a few days before I would leave. They don't have to let you know any sooner than that. The taxpayers pay for your transportation and they pay your salary.

My husband arrived with my daughter the last two days of Basic Training. I only got to see them during our free time which was not much. I cried the first time I saw them. Cry was all I could do since I had not completed training, and there were some things you just could not do. It did not matter that they were my family, and that I missed them. I had to keep my composure while around them until I had completed Basic Training, and I only had two more days to go!

The day came for everyone to get their orders. I got mine. I was going right down the road. Yes, right down the road to Brooks Air Force Base. So, I packed my things, and when I got up the next

morning, we all left. We left going to our assigned
bases for our training. Whatever the training was,
and wherever it was located. Some folks went to the
Airport, others got on buses, and I got in the car with
my family. I headed down the road. It was not very
far at all, probably three or four miles away. It was a
small base, nothing like Lackland. Lackland was
huge. This base was small, and quite relaxed
compared to where I had just come from. I checked in
and was given the building number to report to the
next day at 0800 which is 8:00am civilian time.

The next morning, I reported as instructed and
when I walked in, I walked into a small group of
people. Some had been in the Military for quite some
time. I could tell since they had stripes, some of them
had many stripes. You can tell their rank by the
stripes. Some of them had three or four stripes, and I
only had one. This was a clear sign that I was a
rookie, and everybody knew it. I wasn't by myself,
there were several others that had just come from
Lackland as well. Mostly young men. If I remember
there were only four or five women, and we were
approximately a class of sixteen.

Once again, I was in unfamiliar waters, so I had to tread lightly until I could find my way. The instructors introduced themselves and had each of us introduce ourselves to them and each other. They took us through what we would cover in class. They told us there would be many tests, so we would test for each area we would cover while on the job. The Air Force has since changed the name of this job description. It is now called "Public Health Specialists; Eliminating Preventable Hazards." Below is a brief description:

Whether they're active in the field or performing duties on base, the safety of our Airmen is a top priority. It's the job of Public Health specialists to protect our forces from a vast array of illness and disease by minimizing health risks within our community. Responsible for everything from educating Airmen on safety procedures and food inspection to investigating hazardous materials and sanitary standards, these professionals perform public health activities ensuring that our Airmen remain healthy on bases all over the world.

I found out that we would cover many topics

right down to sexually transmitted diseases. Not that one was running rampant around the base. At that time those were the no, nos. Some were exploring their newfound freedom. The single guys were having fun. Now in today's world we have so many more diseases to worry about. All I can say to that it is best to just be careful. We had no time to play. Those classes were not easy, in fact, they were hard. As class began, reading assignments were issued, and deadlines were given. I can say I didn't have any idea, however I guess being so young may have been my saving grace, because I wasn't scared. I was scared, but not about the "schoolwork". That I knew I could do. My plan was to work hard, and get it done.

While I was getting familiar with my classes and my classmates, my husband found us a quaint little furnished house full of antiques right off the road that led directly into the base. It was a beautiful little place that we could rent while we were there. It was perfect. It had two bedrooms and one bath with a nice living room, and a good size kitchen. Just big enough for us. The man that owned it lived in the house right in front of it. It was tucked behind the main house. We dove right in.

We only had six weeks to get this class done, pass with 80% or better, and move on to our perspective bases to work. We had a few people that did not make it to the end. They left. I guess it was not what they thought it was going to be. The group got a little smaller. As we started to bond, we started to create study groups. We would go over the material together and read aloud to each other. We were getting ready for these tests. Those tests were coming, and there was no leniency. You had to pass in order to move forward.

We went on several field trips on the base. We went to the hospital and spoke to some of the nurses and doctors. One field trip that stands out in my mind was a field trip that ended up being an activity. We went to a tear gas trailer. Yes, a tear gas trailer! Each person was given a tear gas mask, and a protective suit to cover our bodies. We were instructed to put the suit on, hold the mask in our hand, then we had to go inside, while they closed the door. Now the objective was to hold your breath, put on the gas mask, make a seal, and then they would let you out. OMG! Is all I can say to this. Tear gas burns. It makes any exposed skin feel like it is on fire. There were several people that did not make it through this one. They got tear gas under their masks, or they didn't begin to hold their breath in time. Who knows, I just know that they began to cough, and choke uncontrollably. It was quite scary.

Then my turn came. I have no idea how I did it, but I did. I held my breath; I went in and I made the seal on the mask. That didn't mean that my skin didn't feel like it was on fire. All I know is that I could breathe. I wasn't coughing uncontrollably, my eyes were burning, along with my skin being on fire. I made it through one more obstacle. You must know I was praying; I prayed all the way through the exercise. Class moved forward. I do believe that we lost someone else in our class after that exercise. We were told that it was part of our training because if we were to go to war while we were serving, we would be required to go out and assist the hospital with the injured troops, and we would be required to suit and mask up. The thought of it scared me, so what were the chances that it would happen. That one is too hard to call. No one knows. It would be based on circumstances that I had no control over. All I knew was that I would have to comply when the time came.

Luckily, we did not go to War!

My husband wasn't enjoying himself at all. He was not liking that place. It didn't help at all since he didn't know anyone, and he didn't like the fact that I was spending so much time with my classmates. I had to. I had to pass these classes, and how better to do that than with the people who you are in class with. Several people in our study group were having a bit of a hard time, so those of us who had it a little easier were trying to push them along. Teamwork makes the dream work. The dream was passing these classes.

My Dad came to visit me on his way back from seeing family. My Father was from Texas. That is where he was born. He stayed with me a week. It was so good to see him. Remember I had never been away from him more than a few days ever. Yes, I had been to Texas before, no not all of Texas, but I had seen enough. My husband was ready to leave, and when he left, I decided I would send my daughter back with my Dad. I only had about 1 week left of class, and I would be getting my orders to where I would be stationed when I had successfully completed the training.

I had no one to keep my daughter for me while I studied and completed the training. I knew no one in this town. During these times they did not have accommodations for women. If you wanted to be in the Military, you had to figure it out. Our daughter went back to San Francisco my hometown where I was born and raised. I decided for her to stay with my God Mother until I got settled and could send for her. My husband flew to Los Angeles and rode to San Francisco with one of his cousins. Since he wasn't taking our daughter with him, he went to visit family. We packed up our belongings, we said our goodbyes, and everyone left me ten days before class was over.

Classes are over. The last day they give you your total class score on a piece of paper. They don't embarrass anyone, however by this time we all have an idea who struggled. I only remember we had one or two people that didn't pass overall. I think they could repeat the class. Who wanted another 6 weeks of that? I know I didn't. Now when you got your passing score you also got your next assigned base. I ended up going to Sheppard Air Force Base which is in Wichita Falls, Texas. My first thought was, "Am I ever going to leave Texas"?

When I looked on the map (and old fashion paper map) Wichita Falls, Texas is close to the Oklahoma border. I asked myself how I was going to get there, and I reply, by car. They gave me three days to make it there. I had three days to get to Wichita Falls. Those three days felt like a hundred years. I went into the Air Force to get great training, which I had now done. I also wanted to go places I had never been. I had been in Texas for three plus months. I was about to spend the next five years in Texas. OMG! I was feeling a little disappointment. I pack up my belongings, and I head out. I realize I can't drive! I don't have a driver's license.

One of my friends from class that was stationed north of me (I don't remember where) spoke with my husband, and offered to drive me to the base, and we bought him a bus ticket for the rest of his trip. I arrive in Wichita Falls, Texas. I report, and I am given a room in one of the dorms. I took a room in the dorm because it would allow me to find a place to stay on or off base, so that my family could join me.

I was missing my family, I was going somewhere I did not want to be, so right about now I was miserable. They would join me soon, but not soon enough. After I checked into the base, got my room I went with my friend to the bus station and saw him off to his family. I am now in a town where I absolutely know no one. The one person I did know just left me. I went back to the dorm and unpacked my stuff. It wasn't much mostly clothes. My loneliness did not get a chance to last long. Some of the young ladies in the dorm came down and introduced themselves to me. There was a young lady that was the dorm master, and she told us the rules. No men in your room, no loud music, no running, and no young men in your room. Yes, she repeated it more than twice. If you got caught with a man in your room it was a serious infraction. Now, this didn't stop it from happening, however we knew it was something you were not supposed to do. Many would sneak young men into the dorm, some got caught, some didn't.

They showed me around the base so I would know where everything was. I hadn't reported to work yet. I had only had to report on base. We did a lot of walking. No one had a car that I remember except me. I didn't drive. I didn't drive because I didn't have a driver. So, I did a lot of walking. I was in pretty good shape since the whole time I had been in the Military we were exercising, I was walking.

I had been on base maybe three or four days, and it began to snow. By this time, it is late October, and my 20th birthday had passed. I spent that birthday by myself. I remember because I enlisted in May which means I left Basic Training in early August which would have me completing six weeks of classroom training around late October. I see snow for the first time. I had never seen snow! I had only seen snow on television. I went out in the freezing cold and made snow angels, and everyone thought I was crazy. I was in heaven until I started to thaw out. OMG! I had never been that cold in my life. I was born and raised in San Francisco. It didn't get cold there. I never owned a real coat until this time. I had to go buy one unless I wanted to freeze.

I reported to work. I met the other people in the office. Everybody was welcoming. The Master Sergeant that oversaw the office was so sweet. He was a very peaceful soul. He was older probably in his 40's. I never asked, so I am just guessing. The secretary was a young black woman, and she was single. There was a black Sergeant. I remember him well. Why? Because he was extremely angry. He complained about everything and swore that everyone in the office other than me and the other young black woman was prejudice. Everyone else in this office was not of African descent. That I know.

Now my training class was well balanced given there were only sixteen of us. I grew up in San Francisco which is extremely diverse. It was not uncommon for me to be around a diverse group of people, but now I am in Texas. I was learning that things were not quite the same there. This is just ten miles from Oklahoma. I was seeing things I had never seen before. Now I am not saying that I had not felt prejudice. It was just so extremely obvious. Just out in the open. I found myself with this angry man, always complaining, and I had to do my base/site specific training with him.

At this point in my life, I am not accustomed to what I am beginning to experience. I have always had my own opinion, and I have never been easy to influence. The harder you push me, the harder I am going to push back. I was beginning to rebel against his antics. I am not saying that he was not justified in how he felt. I am merely saying I didn't see it the same way that he did. That was just my point of view. The way they were treating me did not reflect that. I was starting to feel like he was part of the problem, and not the solution. Now the Master Sergeant ran a pretty relaxed office. He hardly ever had me go out and do my job. I would always ask, and he would always say let one of the guys do it, so I did. I am following orders. In the Military that is what you do follow orders. I had it made. It would be nothing for me to sit around with my feet on the desk with a magazine. I was bored most of the time.

About six months into my job they moved our office out of the hospital to offices on base just down the road from the hospital. They gave us a building that we shared with the Veterinary Services. They had one side, and we had the other. Before this we were in two separate offices in the basement of the hospital. We were able to spread out, and I was given an office with a window. Twenty-years old with an office, and it has a window. Wow! I was big time.

Well, the shakeup began a few months after the move. Master Sergeant was removed. He retired, and I don't think it was by choice. Not sure why, however somethings you just don't ask. Later I realized it was probably because we didn't ever do much work. He was replaced by a Tech Sergeant, and he was hungry for that promotion, he was going to get it. He was going to get it because he was going to make us work. We were going to do our jobs, and we were going to do them well. I was going to have to go out. I was put in charge of all the inspections of the base facilities. This meant I had to learn how to drive the base van that was assigned to us. I didn't have a clue. It was what we call three on the tree. Which means it was a standard or stick shift, but the stick was on the steering column. Now mind you I do not have a driver's license. It was not a requirement when I enlisted, however it was going to be one now. New boss, new rules.

They would take me out to practice, and my husband and daughter who are back by now of course would help me practice in his car which was also a stick shift. His stick was on the floor. It was not the easiest thing I had to do, but I was going to get it done. Determination had set in by now. I would practice more at work than at home. My husband would take me to work, and he would pick me up. One morning I was running late, and I needed him to hurry up. Well he wasn't moving fast enough, and I was beginning to get frustrated. I grabbed the keys and took the car. Yes, I did, I took the car.

The only challenge I was really having was getting the car to move. Once it moved the other gears were easy to maneuver. I got to work, and everybody realized that I had brought myself, so it became a joke. We lived on base, so I didn't have to go far. The most important thing was I didn't have to try to get on base. The MPs would have arrested me for sure. I was a dead giveaway. I went on my lunch hour and practiced stopping and starting. I got it down. I began to drive myself around in the van at work. Someone would go with me, I would drive. I went and got my driver's license with no trouble. I passed the written test, and the driving test with ease. I was so proud of myself. I was on my way. I could ride around by myself now. I was a big girl.

I had a great job. I enjoyed the work. I

completed the scheduled inspections for the barber shops, beauty shops, swimming pools, cafeteria, etc. I even took culture samples for the ice machines. I was following OSHA, Public Health, and CDC guidelines. Which have followed me throughout my life. Everybody had to comply, and I was the person that made sure they did. I look back on this now, and it was a lot of power for one very young woman to have. I could close anyone of these places in a matter of minutes. I remember one time I went to the barbershop, and there was a young lady working there. I think she was the daughter of the owner. They were not Military, and they did not have to be. It is very common for a civilian to own and operate a business on base.

This young lady was not wearing a smock which is a requirement. It still is. I questioned her about the smock, and the gentleman (white) says to me "she is just helping out today, so can't you just look over it." I looked at him, and since I was not what you would call in a giving mood I said "No, what I can do is go to my next site and come back. If she doesn't have a smock on, I am going to close you down for non-compliance." I did exactly that, and she had on a smock when I got back. From that point on they hated to see me coming. I could see the disgust in their faces when I would come by. I didn't care. I was doing my job, and if I didn't, I would have been in trouble, I would have been the one to be reprimanded, so better they be in trouble and/or closed than me being in trouble.

One time I had to shut down the pool. Yes, in the middle of a Texas summer. The hottest time of the year. My brother-in-law had come to visit us for the summer. He was young at the time. He is about eight years older than my oldest daughter, so he was about fourteen at the time. It was summer, so I had to find something for them to do. My husband was at work as well, however since I worked, and lived on base it was much easier for me to go home at lunch time. I went home and got them so that they could go swimming. Perfect thing to do on one the hottest days of the summer. It had to be over 100 degrees on this day. I told them that when I got back to the office to check my schedule of inspections I would come by the pool and check on them.

I went back to the office and found that the

pool was on my list of inspections for this day. I headed out on my inspections making my way around to the pool. When I got there, I walked in and found the pool operator to let him know that I would be inspecting the pool. I walked around to make sure that lifeguard was in his respective place, and there were enough lifeguards for the number of people who were there, and the pool operating system was in order at the time. Everything seemed to be in order. Now it is time for me to test the water. I am testing the water to make sure that the chemicals are at the correct levels. That is how we prevent bacteria from forming.

This is extremely important especially since on a hot day, and with the large number of people that are there swimming it could be a recipe for a disaster. There could be lots of bacteria floating around. This means that people could get sick, lots of people can get sick. I begin to test, and the pool has almost no chlorine level at all. OMG! I told him "everyone will need to get out of this pool Now!" He was astonished! "He said "all these people paid to be here, what am I going to do?"

What I knew for sure was that no one could swim in that pool period. Not at that time for sure. I told him you are going to have to shock the pool. I went around and began to get the lifeguards to get people out of the pool. Of course, they are asking what is wrong. I didn't say anything. I told the operator to shock the pool, and I would be back in about two hours, and if the levels were where they should be, I would allow the people back in the pool. I've got my daughter, and my brother-in-law looking at me like what's wrong? I whispered to them "the pool is low in chlorine, and you can't swim until it is at the right levels, or you will get sick. They told me that they understood.

I got back in the truck and headed off to do some other inspections and I would come back in a couple of hours. I made it back and noticed that quite a few people had left. I tested the water and told him it would probably be okay in about 15 more minutes. It was not ready yet. I don't think he realized that it was that low. I told him that I would hang around just to make sure. I found a lounge chair to sit in, and I sat there and waited, everyone was on pins and needles. I had the final say as to whether the pool would be closed for the day. It was probably about 3pm currently. I only remember because I know I did not have much longer to work when I got back to the office. The fifteen minutes passed, and it seemed like forever. I retested the water and it was good. He could let those that were still there back in the pool. He was so happy, and thanked me over, and over. I would imagine that he thanked me so many times because I could have shut him completely down, he could have lost the entire day opposed to just losing a few hours, and he would not have been able to reopen until I cleared him.

He managed to get off with just a little slap on the hand. I told him "Just check the chlorine levels more often, especially in this heat, and add chlorine as needed". He was grateful for the advice, so I left. I went back and picked up the kids when I got off work. They were willing to offer up the gossip from the pool telling me that he was really scared and was hoping I did not shut him down completely. He was very, very nice to them of course. All I could tell them was that I was just doing my job.

Then there was the time that I went to the

chow hall at the hospital. Now I always ate lunch at the hospital. They were the best cooks. Everyone came to the hospital. I saw people that I would not see any other time if they did not come to the hospital chow hall.

I went to the hospital on this occasion to check the ice machines for bacteria. I would take ice samples from the dispenser, let them melt then put them in a petri dish to see what they would grow. The hope would be that they did not grow anything. I would expect that they might grow something, just enough not to exceed the allowable limit. Anytime you have machines like that with what could be hundreds of people using them every day, you are bound to have something grow.

This time the culture grew bacteria that exceeded the allowable limit, so I had to go to the chow hall to talk with the manager to tell him that he would have to shut down the ice machine. He would need to shut down the ice machine, clean and sanitize the dispenser area, and then he would be able to start it back up to produce ice, and I would come back when it had produced ice again to re-check it. The manager complied, and he called me when the cleaning had been completed. I went back to check it again, and this time the culture was clean, and I was truly happy. I had used that ice machine so many times, and the thought of nasty ice scared me.

The guy that always complained, and screamed prejudice was gone. He ended up getting transferred to a base in North Dakota. Now I had always heard that if you were difficult and caused a lot of trouble you could end up at a base that was in the middle of nowhere, and Minot, North Dakota is in the middle of nowhere, or at least it was back then. When he re-enlisted for another 4 years, he immediately received orders to report to the base in North Dakota. I was glad to see him go. No love lost there. We had had words about many things, so seeing him go was not hard. Me and everyone else in the office

By this time, we had a new person in the office. He was a Sergeant. He was transferring from another base; he would be doing his last four years at our base and then he would retire. This is where my story changes. This guy harassed me, he sexually harassed me for the four years he was there. I was miserable.

It didn't matter what I said, who I told he never stopped. By now, I had already had my second child which was a girl as well. He said anything and everything you can imagine. He would tell me what he would do to me, and how I would like it. This was long before sexual harassment was added to Title VII.

I told the Master Sergeant that was our manager, and he would speak to him, but it didn't stop him from doing it. Now, we have the pervert. Yes, I am calling him a pervert. We now have another change in the office coming. We have an influx of venereal disease cases, so they open an office in the hospital on the first floor, and they send him there to manage that office.

You can guess who they send with him "Me" oh my goodness I must work in this small office with this pervert, and I cannot refuse to do it. I begged my Manager not to send me, but he said I was the best person for the job. It didn't matter that he harassed me every chance he got. Now he could do it every day, and now there was not anyone else who could hear him. Well I learned quick why they sent me. This guy was not smart at all. I still wonder how he even got this job, because I can't figure out how he would have passed the training.

I later found out that he didn't pass the training, he had so much time in they just put him in our office to fill the spot of the rebel. Well guess who ended up doing all the work. Me! Our job was to do all the case screenings, and report once a month to CDC. Anyone that came in with symptoms was tested. If they tested positive, they were required to come to our office for an interview. Once the interview was completed, we were required to interview them regarding their sexual partners, and then we were required to notify those partners so that they could come in and get tested and treated.

I ended up having to do another type of background check, and I also had to sign several disclosures. I had access to others medical records. I knew information that could not be made public. You get really good at keeping a secret. This job didn't help me make any friends, because deep down people believe that you have told someone their secret. They don't know who, they are just convinced that you have told someone. I never told. I never uttered a word.

Why would I do that? For the trouble I could be in there would be no point. I didn't even begin to try to convince people that I didn't talk. I saw no point.

Now this guy did absolutely nothing in this office except the actual report which he only signed. I would end up doing the report because he did not know how. Most times I would wait until the last minute just to have our Manager yell at him. I did that because it was the only retaliation I had for the sexual harassment. I got pregnant with my third child that ended up being another girl, and this didn't stop him. He kept going. I got so frustrated one day that I told him "If you utter one more word, I am going to leave here and go right to your house, knock on your door, and tell your wife what you are saying to me." He responded with "She won't believe you." My reply to that was "Well let's see, come on get up let's go to your house, and see if she will believe me." He opted not to take me up on this.

He then went from offering up sexual harassment to verbal abuse. It didn't matter anymore. The verbal abuse wasn't any better, but it was easier to tolerate than the sexual harassment. I was trying to be okay with the lesser of the two evils. Both were evil but one just was not as bad as the other in my mind. At the time, I was forced to work with him. I had no choice in where I worked, or who I worked with. I had no recourse, so I had to convince myself of something to survive it. Ask me that question now, and I can tell you the answer is completely different.

I was pregnant with my third child, and I was not having an easy time. I stayed sick the entire pregnancy. I was miserable, misery coming from every direction. I could not catch a break. At some point before most of this happened, I had put in to go internationally. I wanted to be stationed somewhere overseas. Now, I had not heard anything, and it had been at least a couple of years by now. I had forgotten that I had put in for them. Well those orders came. I was to report to Madrid, Spain in 90 days. What am I going to do? I am about five or six months pregnant, by the time I would leave, I would be ready to deliver. What would I do about my Dad? I had learned to be in another state and just see him two to three times a year, but how would I pull this off?

I went to the commander's office to see what
my options might be. I was told that I would have to
take the orders and report to Spain. They may be able
to postpone them until I deliver, but I would have to
go. I would have to go or ask for an early discharge. I
could use my pregnancy as my reason to get out.
During these times we as women did not have many
accommodations. Really, we didn't have any
accommodations. We had to rely heavily on family
outside the Military to help us. We either performed
or we didn't. They didn't seem to take any of these
circumstances into consideration.

I had to decide, and I had to do it quick. There
was no time to ponder over it. I asked for an early
discharge. I ask to leave the Military. Just like that I
gave up my Military career. I received my discharge.
I had until the end of the year. My child was due
Christmas Day, and the Military would cover me until
she was six weeks old. After that I was on my own. It
was over. As simple as a piece of paper, it was over. I
wondered for a long time had I made the right
decision. Who knows if it was or was not the right
decision? All I know is that the right question is
would I be the person I am today? Probably not. It

worked out how it was supposed to.

During my time in the Military, I got my
driver's license, bought my first house at 20, given
birth to two children, and had a wonderful career. I
had gotten away from the sexual harassment and had
to keep people's most personal secrets. I had been
offered a tour in Spain, that I turned down of course.
All before I was 25 years old.   What should I do now?

Before I go, I want you to know that God does not like
ugly. When I left the Sergeant that I worked with got
exposed. He did not get a replacement for me, and
they realized that he did not have a clue what to do,
and that I had in-fact been doing all the work all
along. I could only be replaced by someone that had
the same training since he did not have any. He had
gotten into some financial difficulties as well. They
forced him out early. He ended up with a
dishonorable discharge. He was discharged from the
Military and stripped of his rank.

He wasn't reprimanded for the Sexual
Harassment. I saw him just before he left the base on
a trip to the hospital. All I could do was pity him. I
didn't laugh at him. I had been raised better. I didn't

have to wish him any bad luck, he did that to himself. I held my head high and thought to myself there is a God.

 Driven, yet compassionate Gwen's approach is *"Let's Get It Done Right the First Time."* Gwen believes that communication, coordination, and execution are the three keys to the success in every aspect of life from the smallest to the largest. For that reason, Gwen believes that effective communication is essential to completing any project on time. Knowledgeable, yet approachable, Gwen still finds time to mentor young professionals in both business and life skills.

Because Gwen's passion for service has been her driving force, she believes that women can deliver the same excellence as their counterparts. A Military Veteran, having served in the United States Air Force. With over 25 years' experience in the Construction Industry. Gwen was Business Manager for the Roofers, Water Proofers and Allied Trades Union

Local 136 servicing Metro Atlanta, parts of Tennessee, The Carolinas, Florida, and Alabama. For the last 7 years Gwen has worked on Grant Programs that assist women with obtaining entry into the Local Unions, and Apprenticeship Programs. She continually encourages women to join. Gwen also works with a local Pre-Apprenticeship Program designed for Women introducing them to the Construction Industry. Gwen will provide services and training to the Men as well, however Women receiving quality training along with equal pay is essential. "We can do the work; we just need to be given the opportunity.

$\mathcal{L}$

CHAPTER 5 LISTENING AND LEARNING
James Parks

"Everything today is about listening and learning. Today, I am concerned about the direction that we as a people are headed. We are not putting our good minds together enough to address the problems of climate change, violence, and injustice." In 1969, I was Drafted into the U.S Army after completing High School. I attended Basic Training at Fort Campbell Kentucky, eight and a half weeks of training starting with, learning everything from 1st Aide

Chemical and Biological weapons training and marksmanship, to identifying and disabling landmines, land Navigation, and physical fitness training. I can credit the Leadership Training as one of the best military trainings in the world. I was promoted to PFC (Private first class) after Basic Training.

I attended AIT (Advance Individual Training) at Fort Polk, Louisiana MOS (Military Occupational Skill) 11C40 as an indirect fire crew member. I was trained to operate, maneuver, and provide indirect fire Mortars. The skills required to operate a Mortar Squad consisted of extensive training in map reading, mortar gunnery and fire Direction training. Mortars are used to support the units over all combat mission, my first Duty assignment was in a small Town in South Korea, where my unit was charged to guard the (DMZ) Demilitarize Zone between North and South Korea.

Being in the Army and all the military training gave me the opportunity to serve all over the world. I have had the pleasure of experiencing, first-hand, how people live. Learning the history and culture and serving with some of the best trained professionals in the world has made me a knowledgeable and well-rounded person. It has been an honor and duty to serve my country.

 STAFF Sargent James Parks U.S. Army Retired and lives in Yakima, Washington. As the former President of the NAACP Yakima Chapter, he still remains involved in community justice work and manages to produce an internet-based radio show "Keeping it Real with Sergeant Parks."

𝒰

CHAPTER 6 U.S.M.C. [S1-EP1]
Barry Mixon

The other day I was looking at my tablet and an old episode of Gomer Pyle, U.S.M.C. popped up. When I looked at the title of the episode it said, "Gomer Pyle, U.S.M.C Season One, Episode One *"Gomer Overcomes the Obstacle Course"*, 25 September 1964." The episode opened with Gomer and a couple of fresh new recruits being rushed into a barber's chair by a man in a Marine Corps Drill Instructor's Uniform. I quickly remembered that the man's name was Marine Corps Gunnery Sergeant (GySgt) Vince Carter. As I watched and laughed at some of the scenes, I became oddly aware that I remembered this episode. Not just because it was an old episode from a TV show that I've watched before, but because, it felt more familiar than that.

It was like those old childhood flashback memories you have sometimes. The ones where you somehow clearly remember the "feel" of your first bike ride. You remember how refreshing the wind felt on your face. It was like your skin was brand new and it felt like it happened yesterday. Or the time when I was a kid, living in the Bronx, and there was this massive, thunder and lightning storm. The lightning was so bright and the tremendous rumbling, rolling explosion of the thunder, was so loud, that I truly thought at one point, that if I looked out the window after it was over, the whole neighborhood would be gone.

As I watched the episode, every set, every background felt so familiar to me. I knew what was going to happen next, because I actually lived it. Every scene brought back, a smell, a taste, or a sensation in my body. While I watched the different scenes in the episode, I found that I could still remember the rough texture of the Olive Drab Green Utilities, as they used

about growing up or being anything at all. I grew up in an alcoholic and very abusive household. I am the oldest of five children: three brothers and one sister. My brother Thomas and I have the same father.

My biological father, Leroy Mixon, left my mother when I was only two years old, so I have no real memory of him, except for a very hazy image of him having an argument with my mother at my Grandmother's Manhattan apartment. I don't know what ultimately broke up my mother and father, but my mother never spoke of him... Ever. What I do know is that the relationship left my mother spiritually broken. She never forgave my father and since I was the oldest child, I spent my entire childhood bearing the full force of my mother's pain, anger, and utter contempt she had toward my father.

Remember Smaug, the monstrous Dragon in the book and movie "The Hobbit"? Well, that was Mother on most days. She was beautiful, intelligent and was extremely well read, but alcohol addiction turned her into a fire breathing dragon. Even though I look just like my mother, she only saw my father when she looked at me. I was beaten with whatever weapon or object that she found at the moment, pretty much for sport, and for a long time, I truly thought my name was "Asshole". It wasn't until I saw my birth certificate, that I fully understood that my name was really Barry. I was twelve years old. I have absolutely no memory of my mother ever telling me that she loved me or was even proud of me...Ever. And for years, I had to deal with the fact that she never would. My mother died in 1996.

I was seventeen when I joined the United States Marine Corps, on August 21, 1978. I literally had to beg my mother to sign the paperwork to give me permission to join before I was eighteen. I used a report that I wrote in school on Lincoln's signing of the Emancipation Proclamation as the foundation of my argument to my mother as to why she should set me free. I think the only reason she eventually signed it, was because she liked my creativity, although she would never tell me that. In my mind, I originally thought I would go to college right out of high school, but the application process was far too slow for me. I had to get away from her.

My mother's daily and increasingly abusive

behavior toward me and everything I did or thought of
doing was beyond unbearable. Just the thought of
coming home from college in the future was an insane
concept to me. I had read somewhere that back in the
Vietnam era, people were given the choice between
prison and joining the Marines. One day, I figured
since I was already in prison, well, in Hell really, that
the Marine Corps would be a good place for me. I
didn't know a lot about the Marine Corps other than
the uniforms were cool. There you go. Sold! I just
needed to go somewhere. That's what my Mother used
to say to us all the time, if we even thought about
missing school. She would say, "I don't know where
you're going, but you getting the Hell out of here."

My mother didn't have different colors in her
Crayola box, she had two colors, Black and White.
Grey? No. I considered the French Foreign Legion for
a while. It was an option for me, but it was a little too
far away and I failed French in High School, so I
joined the Marine Corps. I left in the middle of the
night at about 0300 hours, with my Marine Recruiter.
I was so focused on leaving, that I don't remember
anything about him; I couldn't tell you if he was Black
or White. Even after all these years it still feels like a

Dream. The only person I said goodbye to, was my little sister, Jamel, who was nine years old and half-sleeping. I just didn't think that anybody else would miss me.

During the whole trip to Parris Island and throughout the entire 16 weeks of Marine Corps Boot camp, I remember taking great pride in trying to guess how much time would past before they noticed that I was missing. This was easy for me to do since I never received any mail from my family or from anybody really. I would write them, and nothing. The Drill Instructors noticed that I never received any mail, and every Mail Call, they let the entire platoon know that I didn't have anybody. I felt more like a piece of shit than anybody else in the platoon.

It was years before I physically came back home and decades before I was mentally and spiritually able to do so. The United States Marine Corps was the mother I never had and the father that I longed for. Marine Corps Recruit Depot, Parris Island was a very hard experience for me. Not just physically, but mentally too. There were many times when I thought death was eminent, either at the hands of the

Drill Instructors or by something stupid I did. Spiritual depression came late at night, in the form of many, hot, wet tears. There were so many hours at night when I would lie there totally angry with myself and say, "You mean you actually signed up for this madness? "This proves everything that Mom said about you is true. You are so stupid! "You know you could have stayed home for this."

Years later, with decades of experience under my belt as a dad and as a Science teacher, I think the biggest thing that boys and girls are missing are their dads or somebody to be their dad. Dads can just teach you things that you couldn't learn, or it would take a long time for you to learn on your own. The U. S. Marine Corps is the kind of dad, who assumes you know nothing. The Marines strip you down to nothing, whatever you thought you knew, forget it. All the ways and things you used to do, which in the Marines means everything...it's gone. Breathing?? On your own? "Ok Private, the Marine Corps will allow you to do that on a case by case, but only on a need to have basis". The Marine Corps teaches you how to think. At first in a completely controlled environment but later on as you build more and more confidence you start to feel differently.

In Marine Corps Bootcamps, in both Parris Island and San Diego, are where seeds are planted. Sometimes those seeds bear fruit right away, but often-times those seeds germinate years or decades later.

The Marine Corps did exactly what it was designed to do. It gave me the greatest gift that anyone could ever ask for in their lives, a foundation. A sense of belonging to something so much bigger than yourself. As I thought about Season One and Episode One of my show, "*Barry Mixon, U.S.M.C.*" I realized that Marine Corps Bootcamp showed me, that I had possibilities and the potential of being more than who I was told I would ever be. In retrospect, I don't think there is any time in my life, where the Marine Corps didn't play some part in or teach me a lesson or empower me with a technique or a tactic that I could utilize, in order to survive.

In the sixty years, that I have had the pleasure and incredibly good fortune of living, I have been through many "wars". I am a Veteran of countless campaigns and operations; an alcoholic and abusive childhood, three failed marriages, the death of my children, poverty, unemployment, and a year of trying to survive homelessness on the streets of Chicago during the winter of 1992, and on and on. And yet through it all, the sometimes-indescribable pain, and despair, it was the lessons, the difficult and hard-fought lessons, that I learned in that first season in the U.S. Marine Corps, that gave me the strength, the courage, and the intestinal fortitude to carry on. To believe in myself, even in times, and there were many, when no one else did.

I am so proud to be able to say that this year will be the 57th Season of *The Barry B. Mixon, U.S.M.C. Reality Show.* I have learned so much about myself during that incredible journey. I have learned that I actually look better with my head clean shaven. I have learned that words like Teamwork, Pride, Honor, Commitment, Self-Reliance, and Dedication are more than just words put on highway billboards, they stand as testimonies of a decision that I and thousands of other men and women, from every race and background, willingly made so long ago. In all the episodes, that I have lived through, I have learned that like the molecular structure of a substance, those words, those concepts, are essential "Elements" to the very foundation of who I am and how I choose I live to today.

From the moment I raised my right hand and swore to "Protect and Defend the Constitution of the United States from All Enemies, Foreign and Domestic" I became a member of one the greatest fighting organizations that the world has ever seen. I learned over years, that because I heard the "call" like so many others before me have heard over the past 245 years, that the motto "Semper Fi" (Always Faithful), would be like oxygen to my existence.

Best of all, seeing that first episode of **Gomer Pyle, U.S.M.C.** made me realize that I had it all wrong. My mother wasn't just my mom, she was actually part of the show. I just didn't know it then, she was chosen to play the role of Gunnery Sergeant Mom. You know when you arrive at Marine Corps Recruit Depot, Parris Island, at 0400 hours, you are mentally and emotionally exhausted and that strong fierce Drill Instructor, got on the bus, yelling at the top of their lungs, telling us how for the next sixteen weeks they will be your mother and father...that was my mother! I just didn't recognize her in uniform.

I will always be tremendously and forever grateful for the United States Marine Corps for being the family that I thought I never had and more importantly the foundation that provided me the opportunity to be who I am today. After writing this, I now understand why I always get a little emotional when I watch a Marine Corps commercial and hear the words, The Few. The Proud. The Marines.

 Barry B. Mixon is a native New Yorker, a 14-year U.S. Marine Corps veteran, a Biological and Chemical Scientist, a Homelessness survivor, a 5-time Toastmaster International District Speech Champion, an International Science Educator, Gemmological Storyteller, the Chicago Defender's 2020 Man of Excellence and owner of The Gem Hunter Gemmological Appraisals and Storytelling Services. Where he uses the Art, Science, History and Magic of Gemstones, Precious metals, and Fine Jewelry as an "Inception point"; to empower people the world over, to Discover the "Value" of their own Stories.

CHAPTER 7 AN ACT OF SELFLESS SERVICE
Donald Davis

I often wonder how and why I became the man I am, one who cares for my fellow man or woman, wanting all to succeed and become their best person. I knew there was something more to be learned and experienced in order for me to grow into the person I was to be. Joining the United States Army gave me that opportunity.

I had been in the Army for thirteen years when in September 1990 I was deployed to Saudi Arabia during Operation Desert Shield. The Iraqi Army had already invaded Kuwait and were planning to move into Saudi Arabia. Saudi Arabia was an ally. We were planning for war, after all, this is what we trained for, (to serve, protect, and defend our country, including our allies).

As my units Nuclear Biological and Chemical Non-Commissioned Officer, I was responsible for ensuring we could survive a nuclear biological or chemical attack from the enemy and advise the commander on how best to avoid the contamination in order to continue our mission, coordinating decontamination of personnel and equipment if needed.

It was January 17, 1991, the start of Operation Desert Storm. The war started with the air campaign to prevent the Iraqi military from entering Saudi Arabia and pushing the Iraqi military out of Kuwait. We knew they had chemical and biological weapons and had used them on their own people as well as during the wars with both the Soviet Union and Iran. They would surely use them against the U.S. Army and our coalition forces.

What I had learned throughout my military training was surely going to be put to the test. Was I capable and was my unit ready for a chemical or biological attack. As the Iraqi military launched scud missiles into Saudi Arabia our patriot missile battalions intercepted most if not all incoming missiles. Based on the sounds of the explosions, we could tell how close and whether a missile had been intercepted or if one had actually impacted.

As the night progressed into the early morning with the air campaign well under way roughly 2:30am, a new recruit came to see me. He had only been in country a few short weeks, newly assigned to our unit. In the army just six months, fresh out of training and here it is, in a war zone.

He said to me shaking with a nervous voice, Sergeant Davis, can I speak to you. I replied, what do you need private in a tone of voice that would frighten any new soldier. He asked if I would recheck his protective mask, that he was fearful it would not work in the event of a chemical attack. I assured him his protective mask was operational, that I had checked all of the unit's protective mask and they were working as they should, not to worry. He was unconvinced and asked me once again to please check his protective mask, saying, please Sergeant Davis, would you refit my protective to my face to be sure.

Seeing the fear in his eyes as we were hearing the explosions from scud missiles being intercepted, I proceeded to check and refit his protective mask at the same time trying to reassure him that everything would be alright.

He was still unconvinced, he asked if he could have my protective mask. I paused for a moment, looking him in the eyes and asked, why do you want my protective mask, they're all the same. He replied that he wanted mine because he was sure mine worked. I was an experienced soldier, he was a new soldier and unsure of his limited training, he asked, do they really work, will they protect us from a chemical attack. I informed him that in fact I had worn my mask in a chemical environment and they do work.

Without giving it any thought, I gave this young soldier my protective mask and took his mask for myself. Thinking, if that's what he needed to feel secure, then that was the right thing to do. Seeing the relief on his face will forever stay with me. It was a feeling that's not easily explained. One I had not experience before, but it was good and I wanted to hold on to it. For that brief moment I forgot we were at war.

Thankfully, because of the overwhelming force of the air campaign, the Iraqi military was unable to use the chemical weapons against us. We went on to faithfully serve our country and this young soldier performed to the highest, with confidence and a willingness to take on any task given. For me, it was the greatest test, it showed me who I am.

I tell this story because although it may seem simple, it represents who I am and had it not been for my service in the U.S. Army, I may not have realized what I was capable of as it relates to my fellow man. You see, serving in the any branch of service for our country means we serve all in our country, no matter the cost.

Serving in the United States Army For more than 20 years brought out what was always there, **An Act of Selfless Service**, I continue to try and live by that daily and always pray that I can make a positive difference in the life of another, caring for my fellow man or woman, no matter the cost.

"Greater love has no one than this, that one lay down his life for his friends."

John 15:13

Donald Davis

Sergeant First Class

United States Army (Retired)

Donald is 63 years of age and was born in Camden, S.C. and raised in Brooklyn, N.Y. where he entered the U.S. Army in 1977.

Donald currently resides in Marietta, Ga with his wife of 37 years. They have one son aged 35. Donald is very active in his church and has been employed by the Kroger company as an assistant store leader since 1999.

𝔐

CHAPTER 8 MY ARRIVAL TO A PLACE UNKNOWN
Veronica Gadsden

Always Let God Lead You and You Shall Be Victorious!

My preparation for the journey was to tell my sons, I had to go to war. So, I called them up and explained that the day was coming for my departure, in telling my 17-year-old, his statement: "you gotta do what you gotta do". My five-year-old response was: "will you be back"? With tears in my eyes and the confident in God, I assured him that I would return, and my journey began.

Upon my arrival in Saudi Arabia late on

January 29, 1991 and being transported to an area where we would rest for the night, an emergency announcement came, and we all had to put on our MOPP gear (that's when there could possibly be a gas attack). Now, I was more scared than ever before being on unfamiliar ground. But there was one thing I did know as a child of God, I was protected and that was how I made it through the months of Desert Storm in Southwest Asia (SWA). Once we were settled in our living area, in which I, the overseer of at least 20 women (who looked to me for guidance), God gave me guidance to do so. I would rise early and worship and meditate on God's word to be ready for the duties of the day. In doing so, it prepared me to be closer to God and having the assurance that I would be returning home.

I did not know how long I would have to be in that environment, but God had a plan for me in my months in the desert. I was a true witness for the Lord, giving assurance that we would be returning home soon. My confidence came by trusting in God, knowing I could do all things when I kept him first. I knew that my God had not brought me to Saudi Arabia only to leave me.

As time moved on and one of my assignments was being on the Litter Team. The "Litter Team" was a team of six or more soldiers who would be on standby to transport the injured, once brought in my helicopter. That dreadful day came, and the call for the Litter Team rang out, as we ran quickly to the receiving point to transport the injured soldier from the helicopter. Once in the emergency room (which was a tent like M.A.S.H☺) I then realize a war had begun. I began to pray for the young man who was hit while in his tank. Seeing the injured soldier made me realize a war had truly begun.

While Desert Storm was announced as one short war, lasting only 100 hours, it was truly an experience of a lifetime. I held onto God's unchanging hand and knew that as long as I held him close to me and He held me, I would be alright. I didn't think I could make it but I held onto the word of God and whenever I felt stressed his word would be recalled. Though my experience in SWA was one of growth in God, I would not want to experience leaving my family again. I always began my day with prayers and ended it with writing in my daily journal and always thanking God for another day's journey. I am grateful that He saw something in me that I did not see in myself. I realized that through it all with His strength, anything is possible.

The memories that will always be with me, I left my two sons five and seventeen, my family, a newborn granddaughter and returned to a blessing of a nephew, born on the day of my arrival back to the states(home). What a mighty God I serve! I thank God for allowing me the experience of a lifetime and safely returning home. Isn't God Good! Always remember Phil 4:19 - But my God shall supply all your (my) needs according to his riches in glory by Christ Jesus.

$\mathcal{F}$

CHAPTER 9 1ST SQUAD 3RD PLATOON
JW Bob Belcher

First Squad Third Platoon, Company L Third
Battalion, 395th Infantry Division, 99th

Division, U.S. Army

A friend asked me the other day why I don't talk about
my World War II days. I said I don't think anybody
would be interested, he said he would.

Back in 1946, nobody seemed to believe
anything I said about it so I stop talking about it. I
have written a little bit about my life history including
the Army for my immediate family, but there's a lot of
stuff I doubt anybody would want to hear outside of

family. I'll just write about my Army days from registering for the draft to "hello folks, I'm home."

On November 22, 1943, I reached my 18th birthday. The government said, "you are supposed to register." I did and sometime in March 1944, I received an invitation to go to Camp Forest near Tullahoma, Tennessee for a free physical examination. Along with a bunch of guys aged 18 to 38, including Bill Monroe, who became a little bit later known as the king of bluegrass music, caught a bus to Camp from Nashville Tennessee. I passed, Bill didn't. He sang all the way back to Nashville.

They had us all strip off everything. A whole bunch of naked men in a small gymnasium. I'd never seen an uglier sight. Some were bragging, some trying to hide. We went back to Nashville with orders to be at Union Station to catch a train to where, we didn't know. A day or two later we unloaded at Camp Shelby, Mississippi near Hattiesburg. We were there a few days just listening to lectures, etc.

I remember a corporal came into the barrack and asked if there was any light truck drivers. A lot of hands went up including mine. He said follow me. The truck had one wheel and two handles. We hauled Mississippi red clay to fill a hole and a few days later we started our second train ride.

They still didn't say where we were going. After riding a day or two, we got off the train at Camp Walters near Mineral Wells, Texas. There we received seventeen weeks of basic training. Infantry training is a little rough even for teenagers. Along about the end of the seventeen weeks we had to take a twenty-mile hike with full filled packs.

If you could finish up with the captain (Myers) you would receive a 10-day furlough and transfer to Camp Maxey, Texas for prep to go to war. I took my ten days at home and took another train ride to camp Maxey near Paris, Texas.

I joined the 99th Division. I can't remember

how long we were there. We trained and did all the things that armies do. We had passes to Paris and Hugo Oklahoma. Then our orders came down to prepare for another train ride. We boarded trains having no idea where we were going. A few days later we unloaded at Camp Myles Standish near Boston, Massachusetts.

We went through the same old stuff, but this time they issued clothing and equipment needed to go to war. They gave us passes into Boston. I visited China Town, what a sight for a country hick like me.

A few days there they said get everything you own and let's go find a ship. I had mixed feelings about that but the Army makes up your mind for you. We boarded ship on September 30th at Boston Harbor. We didn't know our destination until we docked at Plymouth England. I think I'm right about Plymouth. From there we were transported to Camp Marabout near Dorchester.

This was around the 10th of October and while we were there, we trained and played football. We enjoyed ham that somebody stole off the ship. We had passes to Dorchester. They serve beer and fish and chips and we played darts. Virgil Wadley and I went into town together. Wadley was later killed not more than a few feet from me in a place near Remagen, Germany. I still think about him at times. He killed a cow one time and cooked every man in the squad a steak before cooking one for himself.

We were in Dorchester until about the 1st of November. We took our second ship ride across the English Channel arriving at Le Havre, France around the 3rd of November. The ship anchored down quite a distance out. Barges came along side of the ship. A 10 x 30-foot ladder was thrown over the side. Climbing over that rail and down into that barge with all the equipment wasn't too much fun. One guy yelled, "look out below!" He dropped his rifle. I heard it bounce off of somebody's helmet. The barge went towards shore until it hit sand, then let down the gate. We ran out in five feet of ice water to shore. We walked ourselves almost dry and then was picked up by 6 x 6 trucks.

This was sometime in the evening. It was dark and cold. We rode until it must have been around 4 a.m. We were in Belgium. They unloaded us in a cow pasture, where we pitched our two-man pup tents. We soon discovered we were in a lot of cow dung. At about 6 a.m. we were woken for breakfast. I didn't have the stomach for it but didn't know when we'd eat again. We soon got aboard the trucks and headed east. The next stop was in a pine thicket and it was raining. We pitched tents and took turns on guard. We were called for breakfast. This time we got back on the trucks with no tops. They said that was in case we had to get out fast.

It was cold and wet. The rain had turned to snow. Our next stop, if I remember correctly, was in a pine lot. We pitched our tent in a foot or two of snow. We took turns standing guard all night. It was beginning to get scary. German artillery was flying overhead to the West. American artillery to the east. Up ahead, it look like a big storm was brewing. It was war. That's when I missed home more than any time before. As usual they called us for breakfast. This time transportation was halftracks. Two wheels in front and tank like tracks on the rear. Twelve men could ride in the back with one man and the driver in front. It was very cold. We were nervously shaking and shivering. After a while the halftracks stopped. The driver said this is as far as I go. You'll have to walk the rest of the way.

We trudge through deep snow in a column of tows into a little village called Hofen. Our squad stopped in the middle of town at an old dairy building. The outfit we received had dug foxholes. I now have a great respect for foxes, groundhogs, and gophers, since I learned how they live in the ground. The snow stayed on the ground the whole winter. We were mostly on defense and going on nightly patrols. One of our Sergeants, Charles Murray was killed on a patrol and I think one of our men shot him because of a misunderstanding of the password. Robert Thrasher, one of our most loved buddies was beside him out front on patrol and help bring him back to the CO. It wasn't a life-threatening wound but because of the great distance they had to carry him in the snow, he died on the way.

I don't know how I was lucky enough to get a pass to Paris. I think it was three days sometime in December. When I came back it was the same way into Hofen as the first time. As I was coming up the hill I met a bunch of men running toward me with their hands clasped behind their heads. I thought what the heck! Then I noticed a couple of guys behind them with rifles taking them to a prisoner holding place.

The Battle of the Bulge started. We held Hofen and killed and captured a lot of Germans. I'm not so proud of it but we had to do it. Sometime after the Bulge was over, we went back to Belgium for a ten- or twenty-day rest. We enjoyed good food and showers in the home of some of the Belgium families. It was the first bath for a long time. You can imagine how we looked and smelled. It's been 64 years and I forgot a lot of what we did between there and Remgen (Ludendoff) Bridge over the Rhine.

I do remember that we had come quite a distance one day. We made it into town without any resistance. We were walking along with tanks running along with us. A sniper in a church steeple started shooting at us as we hit a ditch, the squad leader told us to jump out and run back into town. I took off, after about a few steps I ran into a pit full of rotten turnips. I smelled terrible for the next several days. I remember a German tank was running across an intersection up ahead of us at the same time. Wayne

Dean, we call him Gengz Dean, jumped up on our tank and started firing the fifty-caliber machine gun at the tank.

The tank crew said that the tracer bullets that were in the clip helped them zero in on the tank, but he got away behind some trees. When we got to the Remagen, the Ludendorff Bridge had been captured. Shells were still falling and dead Germans and Americans were lying around. We had to watch for big holes in the bridge when we crossed. The next thing I remember was being up on a mountain above the bridge. We didn't see it fall. One day we saw it, the next day it was in the river. Wadley captured a German officer in a barn next to the house we were holed up in for a while. He took a Lugar from him and I was carrying it for him when he was killed. When we got orders to advance, Wadley and I were scouts, so we were in the lead.

We were going down some kind of road or trail and a column of two on each side of the road. A tree had been cut down and was lying across the road. I went around on the left, Wadley on the right. As soon as we were around the tree I spotted two figures

coming towards us. It was nine or ten at night but
there was a little bit of light shining through the trees.
I yelled down! I don't think Wadley saw them. One of
the sergeants behind me thought I was just scared. He
said, "Belcher you didn't see anything!" I was scared
but I knew I saw at least two people walking in our
direction not more than two or three hundred feet.
Wadley stood up and yelled (komm zie her); they
opened up. He was hit bad and died. I was hit in the
shoulder but not a serious wound. I don't really know
what hit me. I have thought maybe what hit me went
through Wadley first. If that was so, the Germans
would have had to go into the woods to our right and
their left.

I stayed in a German House part of that night
until an ambulance took me in black out across the
Rhine. Somewhere they put me on a (DC3 I think) and
flew me to Birmingham, England. Several other
wounded were on the plane. After a few days in the
hospital they released me and gave me a pass to
London. I was on one of those little train somewhere,
I don't remember where, on my way back to the outfit,
when the war ended. I found the outfit somewhere
around Hammelburg and Elfershausen, not too far

from Frankfurt. The next move I made after quite a while and occupation was a Camp Lucky Stripe to wait for time to come home.

I had a job driving officers here and there. One job was transporting a lieutenant to Paris for a weekend. He went his way, I went mine. There I was promoted to Corporal. I don't remember how long I stayed at any of these places. Sixty-four years is a long time. Finally my number came up and I boarded the Sea Corporal to New York Harbor, from there to Camp Atterbury, Indiana. I was discharged and put on a Greyhound to Nashville. I rode my dad's Studebaker to Route #1 Hermitage, Tennessee. I was glad we whipped Hitler. There was a lot of in-between things I could have written about and if I were to write a book I would insert it. I guess you could call this an essay I hope whoever reads it can enjoy what it is essaying.

Sincerely, Possum Town Senior Citizen, Bob Belcher born November 22, 1926

Possum Town was a place my family and I suffered through the 1929 depression.

Please excuse the bad spelling. It took me 9

years to get an eighth-grade education.

Bob has been many things since the war. A carpenter, truck driver, band member, Church Deacon, and a great, great, great grandfather. He has four children. Ronnie, Wanda, Donnie, and Gail. Bob played the harmonica, banjo, steel guitar, guitar, and mandolin. He often said he needed to concentrate on one but somehow it never did.

He and his wife Corrine were married for seventy-four years. Bob passed on April 12, 2021. J W is his name but don't call him that. And no, J W are not his initials. Go figure.

ABOUT PA-PRO-VI PUBLISHING

The owner and founder of Pa-Pro-Vi is LaQuita Parks. Pa-Pro-Vi means pain, progress, victory because we believe that without pain there is no progress and without progress there can be no victory. We help people take their stories from a "thought to a realization!" We are located in the Riverdale, Georgia area. Contact us through our website at www.paprovipublishing.com

Made in the USA
Columbia, SC
30 October 2021